The
Book One

By
Joshua Griffith

ISBN: 978-1-7350784-1-0

Cover art by SelfPubBookCovers.com/ Viergacht

Contact Joshua Griffith on Facebook

Follow him on Twitter

Or on BookBub

Table of Contents

Chapter One

Chapter Two

Chapter Three

Chapter Four

Chapter Five

Chapter Six

Chapter Seven

Chapter Eight

Chapter Nine

Chapter Ten

Chapter Eleven

Chapter Twelve

Chapter Thirteen

Chapter One

In an undisclosed facility along the borders of Russia and China, 1980.

Smoke permeated the cold concrete room as several military officers and government officials paced, waiting for results. Each officer hailed from different countries, representing their respective governments, though not officially. The facility wasn't on the map, let alone on any of the official government-sanctioned lists. It was a ghost that none acknowledged and a place where few ventured to, willingly.

The room itself was sparse, no windows or any furnishings. The men spoke in hushed but worried tones, save one. He stood a towering six foot six, smoking an expensive imported cigar. He stroked his thick beard repeatedly, out of habit, and tapping one of his mirror-shined boots.

"Will this be any longer?" one of the other officers asked nervously, "My boss said not to return unless I had something substantial to report. We can't fail again."

"If your superiors think that *they* can speed the process up any faster," a short lithe woman answered from her squatting position on the floor, "then perhaps you should have them come here and do this themselves!"

"Can you do it or not?" An Asian officer growled, his hand touching the sidearm at his hip, "You can be permanently replaced like all others before you."

"Might be for the best," another officer chimed in, his German accent heavy, "Conjurers can't be trusted to get the job done."

"Really?" The woman eyed her doubters with scorn, "If that were true, then how did you come by all the supernatural creatures here in your little menagerie of horrors?"

"Silence, heathen!" an American in an expensive suit commanded, "Your very presence makes my skin crawl. Do this Devil worship rite and be done with it!"

"Funny how *I* can make your skin crawl, but the use of dark magic doesn't cause you any concern. It should. If I do this correctly, then you best clench that cross around your thick neck tightly. I'm not sure that I can contain it for long."

"Just do your part," the bearded behemoth stated calmly, "My men will deal with it when it arrives."

The woman stood up with a jar of fresh blood/mud, mixing in an assortment of herbs with a paint brush. She purposefully walked around the room, adding different sigils along the walls while softly chanting. The men in the room grew silent, a sense of foreboding engulfed the room as thick as the smoke.

"What evil are you surrounding us with, witch?" The American hissed as he glared at the woman.

"If this *scares* you, Johnson," the bearded officer goaded, "you can run back home and hide under your mother's skirt."

"I'm not scared, Sergei," Johnson indignantly replied, sneering as he pointed at one of the blood sigils, nearly touching it, "I don't like the idea of having my soul damned for all eternal by being a part of this unholy ritual."

"You know nothing of what's holy and what's natural, comrade," Sergei replied as he grabbed his arm, pulling him back.

"Nothing about this is natural! I, for one, believe that this isn't going to end well for any of us."

"What's the point of the art work?" The German asked, feeling uncomfortable as one of the sigils seemed to pulsate.

"Protection." The woman stated, "I'm taking extra precautions with this summoning than the other ones performed here."

"Why?" the Asian officer asked, his English broken, "Nothing went wrong with other rites. Why change now?"

The woman stopped and looked at the men in the room carefully. *Were these men in the loop or just figureheads for their governments?* She glanced over at Sergei, who nodded slightly, giving her permission to speak freely.

"All the creatures we've summoned thus far pales in comparison to what we're calling upon tonight. Tonight, we shall summon a God..."

Murmurs and gasps filled the room, Johnson had an incredulous look, "Seriously? *You* are going to summon the one and only God? You people are so twisted and perverse if you think you can do that."

"Not the Judeo-Christian God, silly boy," the woman giggled as she walked by Johnson. She dotted him on the top of his nose with the paint brush, causing Johnson to jump back in disgust while wiping his nose, "I will be calling upon Babalú-Ayé, a God of disease that *your* people want to force into servitude. These sigils are to keep him weak and drain his power."

"Blasphemy! There's only one God -"

"Johnson," Sergei interrupted the American's rant, "don't let your moral beliefs cloud your judgement. It's a necessary evil, but it's one that is essential to our plan. Each creature in this facility has special traits that will ensure that-"

"We'll all burn in Hell!" Johnson shouted, spittle sprayed from his lips, "The ultimate weapon isn't worth our souls, is it?"

"This isn't your call, Johnson." Sergei got into Johnson's face, the cigar smoke burning his eyes as puffs of smoke assailed him, "We're all here for a purpose, not to question the plan. I don't care where my soul goes, *if* I have one. I'm here to get results from this place by any means necessary. Stop your childish crying or leave this place, but know this: I won't be held responsible for the financial losses your government will incur if you depart. Trust me, there's a lot of money and power at stake, enemies don't last long. You don't want to be on *that* list because you will be dead before your plane touches American soil. Got it?"

"Are you threatening me?"

"No, just stating the facts. Either we succeed or die trying, that's all that matters. Money is not an issue, but results are. Some powerful and influential people are involved with this operation. It's a long-term game that will take time before it bears lasting results that will meet with our respective governments agendas."

Johnson backed away, glancing at the other men. Each one nodded, knowing the price of the project, "How much longer until she's ready?"

Sergei looked over at the woman, who was back on the cement floor, painting more sigils and other elaborate markings. A circle of black salt surrounded her work with a small gap missing.

"Well, Jasmine?"

She looked over her shoulder and replied, "Just a few more minutes. I'm trying to ensure that I didn't forget anything."

"Can we help you?" The German officer asked tentatively.

"All I need to do is light these candles, close the circle, and compel Babalú-Ayé to come forth."

"Good," Sergei turned to the group and commanded, "it's time to vacate the room. My men will need all the extra space to trap this being once he's weakened enough. Head to main commissary. There's food and drinks prepared as well as monitoring screens so that you can watch everything unfold safely. Lt. Gremm?"

A short but stocky soldier entered the room, saluting, "Yes, General?"

"Escort our *guests* to the commissary and have the containment unit be at the ready."

"Yes sir!" Lt. Gremm replied as he saluted once more, then motioned for the government officials to follow him. As everyone was leaving, Johnson locked eyes with Jasmine, "God save us all if this goes terribly wrong."

"If it does," Jasmine replied coldly as she moved around, lighting the candles, "*your* God won't make it here in time for us heathens. Babalú-Ayé isn't a strong God but he still is a God. He might not like being *volunteered* to aid us."

Johnson wearily nodded as he stepped out of the room. The General walked over and inspected Jasmine's spell work. It was beyond his comprehension as to what the symbols did and their meaning, but that didn't detract from his duty as the leader of this ghost facility.

"Do you believe this God will do as we say?"

"Depends," Jasmine answered as she lit the last candle. She grabbed a thick sack and poured more black salt around the circle, closing it and making it thicker, harder to break.

"Why summon him when we could use the rift downstairs? Wouldn't that be easier to use instead of all this?" The General questioned the woman. Experiments had been conducted in this facility for many years, such as human and animal testing in relation to the supernatural. Seeing how demon possession worked, how inter-dimensional travel occurred and if it were possible to do, as well as what actually existed from folklore and legends and how to exploit these creatures.

Five years ago, a group of scientists managed to gather enough information from various entities to literally rip open a hole into the void. It gaped open in the middle of the main substation, letting many different types of creatures spill in. Many people died before the creatures were properly contained, as a result. It was now locked down and closely monitored because one never knew what would come through next.

It was now the facility's best option for pulling entities to this dimension because it gave little resistance. One entity let it be known that Earth has a thick veil surrounding it, making it both difficult and discomforting to travel here from other places and dimensions. The gaping hole in the veil represented a simple way into this world.

"Like I said, this is a God. I'd rather play it safe than leave it up to chance with the rift. What if we compel Babalú-Ayé to come through it and he calls for help, using the rift as a floodgate for an incursion?"

"He can do that?" The General spoke, surprised that something like that could be possible. He snatched a radio from his belt and ordered, "Squads Green and Blue. Cover the hole and shoot anything on sight."

"*Copy that, General!*" Came back over the radio.

"I'm not certain, but we've never dealt with a God before. Better safe than dead." Jasmine replied as she gathered up her summoning supplies. Sergei grabbed her by her arm and asked, "Do you think we can get him to fix the hole?"

"General, all I know is that this is a God. One that won't be here willingly. He may not help at all, unless we give him something in return."

Sergei narrowed his eyes, "What does that mean?"

"Offerings and or a sacrifice," as the General squeezed her arm tighter, Jasmine painfully added, "Think of it as payment for services rendered."

"I don't make deals with *monsters* and I certainly won't pay them *anything*."

Jasmine yanked her arm free, the bruises were already showing, "I get that, but we may not have a choice. If he requires a life, I've already offered one to him."

The General chewed on his cigar roughly, angered by her words, "What! When did you do this treacherous act? Speak, conjurer! Have you been colluding with the enemy?"

"I did it in front of everyone here, when I placed the blood on Johnson's nose. He will make a fine candidate for a sacrifice, if Babalú-Ayé demands one. I'm keeping our options open and for your information, I haven't been talking to '*the enemy*', as you say. If I had, I'd have better information for you than I have now.

Sergei grumbled, "When will the ritual begin?"

"Momentarily," Jasmine stated as she adjusted her blouse, tucking it into the waistband of her black dress, "I need one more item and then I will begin the rite."

As Jasmine rifled through her satchel, Sergei extinguished his cigar and pulled out a new one. He bit the tip off and spat it on the floor, as he reached into his chest pocket for a book of matches, the General had a creepy sensation of being watched.

Normally it didn't bother him, with the plethora of entities within the facility, it was common to feel watched and glared at, but this was different. Sergei lit a match after several attempts and puffed on his cigar nervously. His eyes darted around the room, the only thing he saw was Jasmine walking towards the circle on the floor wielding a small dagger.

The woman took a moment to close her eyes and breathed deeply several times. The General couldn't help grazing his eyes over her small form, watching intently as her breasts hypnotically moved with each breath. He stroked his beard, imagining many lewd scenarios involving the two of them. Jasmine opened her eyes, focusing on the containment circle as she chanted softly, charging it with energy.

Jasmine held out the dagger, pointing it up at the ceiling. She made several swiping gestures, like she was carving patterns in the air. The woman glanced at the General and asked, "Are you sure you want this? There's no turning back once I perform the incantation."

"We have no choice now. Our governments want results, even if it means death. Proceed, Jasmine."

Jasmine could sense the General's trepidation, but it wasn't her place to question it. She had her own reservations about this ritual, never summoning a deity before now gave way to doubts in her mind. Would the sigils work? Is the black salt circle strong enough to contain a God? Jasmine projected an air of confidence in her posture, but in truth, she was shaking like a tree in a hurricane internally.

Jasmine mentally snapped herself back to the task at hand. She pointed her dagger directly at the salt circle, forcefully cried out in Latin, "*Babalú-Ayé, Iubeo te prodire compellunt! Babalú-Ayé, Iubeo te prodire compellunt! Babalú-Ayé, Iubeo te prodire compellunt!*"

The room shook violently as an eerie humming sound assailed their ears. Jasmine strained as she repeated her chant, sweat glistening on her visage. Every sigil in the room glowed, pulsating at times as the room temperature dropped at least twenty degrees. In the center of the circle, a dark shade appeared and slowly took on a humanoid form.

The figure grew in size, standing almost nine feet tall, its girth almost engulfed the salt circle. Jasmine feared that she miscalculated her measurements, wondering if her circle would be big enough to hold the deity. In the blink of an eye, the deity's form morphed, changing to a more realistic version of a human as its features took shape.

The deity wore a full body cloak that shimmered like twinkling stars and was barefoot. Jasmine wasn't sure if it had any other clothes on or had any concealed weapons hidden behind its cloak, but being this close to the God, she felt cold. His face was pale, with no discernable flaws, and long flowing hair that changed colors as the light hit it in certain angles.

The deity took in a deep breath, held it for what seems like forever, but when he exhaled, his eyes opened. The orbs were a shade of black that Jasmine never knew existed and she felt like their roles had been reversed. Never in her life had she felt so small and insignificant until now.

Chapter Two

The General stepped up beside Jasmine, nudging her, "Is this him? Is this the God we need?"

"I think so," Jasmine answered in earnest.

"You mean you don't know?" Sergei growled, his lips fumbling to keep his cigar in place, "How can we be sure that he's the correct one?"

"It's not like I've met a God before, so give me a break!" Jasmine hissed but turned her attention to the deity, "Babalú-Ayé, can you hear me?"

Silence.

"I said-"

"I heard you the first time, witchling!" The deity bellowed, causing both his captors to cover their ears, "You take me for a deaf fool! Why have you brought me here to this dreary place?"

"You're here to answer questions and provide information that we need." Sergei commanded, but took a step back as the celestial being's eyes focused on him.

"Why should I?" It chuckled, which sounded both melodious and ominous at the same time, "You have no idea *who* you are addressing."

"Babalú-Ayé," Jasmine answered, but wondered why she got a nagging feeling that wasn't his name, "please, I implore you to help these men. What will it take to get your cooperation?"

Sergei growled as he lifted his arm to backhand the witch but froze mid swing when the God menacingly threatened, "Hurt her and I *will* level this place with just a thought."

Jasmine moved away from the General, debating on breaking the circle, when Sergei grumbled, "I don't negotiate with the vermin here, you are my prisoner so it is *I* who gives the orders here. Your threats are useless since we both know that you have no power here."

The deity surveyed the room, "Commendable sigil work. Babalú-Ayé would approve the fine details. You are talented."

Jasmine cheeks flushed slightly, but something that the deity said caught her attention.

Babalú-Ayé would approve the fine details.

Before Jasmine could reply, she heard a voice inside her head, "*Don't fear me. Play along and you may yet live through this.*"

Bewildered, Jasmine observed the deity as he roared as he collapsed on the floor. He clutched his chest as he panted, like it was difficult to breath. The deity's head snapped up, lips curled back, revealing several rolls of razor-sharp teeth.

"Release me or I will end all of you... slowly." The God snarled.

"Not until you agree to assist us with our plights," the General kneeled down by the circle, smirking as he blew smoke at the beleaguered God. "Those sigils, as I'm told, are rendering you powerless. So, I suggest that you cooperate *if* you ever want to leave this place."

"Bold talk for a mortal," the God eyed the General, "What is it that you want from this one? It had better be worth the pain."

"So, will you cooperate if we let you out of this little trap?"

"Yes," the deity hissed coldly, causing both the General and the witch to shiver uncontrollably. Sergei looked over his shoulder and barked, "Extraction team, you have a green light."

A group of six soldiers marched into the room, one of the men held a pair of metallic shackles.

"I expect you to wear these," the General pointed at the shackles, "I can't have you causing problems."

"Agreeable," the deity stated as he stood up, "now break the circle so we can be done with this."

Jasmine stepped up to circle. She looked around at everyone, stalling. Uncertainty plagued her thoughts but were interrupted by a voice in her mind, "*I won't hurt you, Jasmine. I swear to you, now break the circle, please.*"

The woman gasped as she ran the tip of her boot through the salt, breaking it. She scurried out of the way as the soldiers moved in to physically restrain the otherworldly entity. Jasmine watched as the God refrained from struggling, appearing to be obedient.

"Good man," Sergei announced as he inspected the God closer, "if you're not too worn out from the sigils, follow me."

"I'm hardly a Man and you will do well to remember that," the deity replied as he noticed that the same sigils and other symbols were crudely etched into his restraints, "Your doing, Jasmine?"

"No, not all of them," the woman replied, "they were-"

"That's classified, so stow it woman!" The General snarled, "Your work is done for now. Go eat and rest. I'll let you know when your services are required."

Jasmine meekly walked away but before she stepped out of the room, she noticed that the God was watching her. He even winked slightly, or was that her imagination? The facility commander stepped in front of the deity, blocking his view as the witch left.

"My name is-"

"Sergei Petrovich, General in the Russian military, overseer of this place. I know who all of you are and..." The deity paused with its eyes closed, then smiled, "what you have hiding here, or should I say what beings are held captive here."

"Cute trick, what else do you know?"

The God smirked, "That's classified, as you say."

Sergei grumbled to himself, "Follow me."

The General walked ahead of the escort down a long, narrow corridor that had doors every ten feet. The deity smiled ever so slightly, sensing the other beings around him. The group rounded the corner where the doors were sporadic, but bullet proof windows gave a view into each room. They all seemed alike: a metal table with rungs in the middle and three folding metal chairs.

Each room had white walls and flooring; some were dirtier than others from use. The General stopped at a red door that had an electronic lock. He swiped a badge and as he held the door opened, Sergei asked, "Down here we have a problem. One I believe you can fix for us, yes?"

"Elaborate please."

"It's classified," the General answered as he walked down a long set of grated steps.

"You seem stuck on that term. If it's classified, then why are you showing it to me? Do these men know about it or can you not discuss it in front of them?"

"It's classified and yes."

Everyone was quiet as they descended into the facility, the clacking of boots echoed throughout the eerie stairwell. The General reached into his pants pocket and retrieved a small piece of paper with the God's name on it. Sergei had difficulty trying to say the name ever since the witch told him about the deity.

"BabalAyé," Sergei fumbled with His name as the group reached the bottom. He pointed ahead, "Do you see the door that's heavily guarded?"

"Is that classified as well?" The deity mocked, "Can I go now? I tire of the secrecy."

"You and I will be going in there, alone. I will tell more about the contents of the room that's not meant for the ears of these soldiers."

"I can barely keep my excitement in check," the God sarcastically retorted with an unreadable visage, "Lead on."

The two teams guarding the door snapped to attention, saluting the General as he and his prisoner marched by. The escort soldiers clustered with the other units as the General turned with his hand on the door handle, "Keep a sharp eye on us. If this one tries anything, shoot him."

Each soldier nodded, checking their weapons. The deity grinned at the men, unnerving them without saying a word. The duo walked into the room that had seen better days. The concrete floor was sticky and stained various shades of brown and black. Countertops connected to three of the four walls, glass door cabinets were both above and below, with various supplies in them.

In the middle of the room sat a metal contraption, it was covered in the same black and brown stains. It had two conical appendages, one attached to the bulk of the machine, the other was suspended in the air, bracketed to the ceiling. Nestled in between them in the air was a gaping hole that swayed and shimmered.

"This *spot* before us has been vexing us for some time now. Do you know if it's possible to seal it?"

The deity looked at the hole and impassively commented, "You people tore a hole the veil and can't fix it. Why am I not surprised? How did you manage this?"

"It's classified."

"If you say that again," the God threatened, "I'll keep tearing it until you can't contain what comes through. I thought that you said that we would talk openly without the ears of the common soldier hearing us in here."

"So, it is possible to manipulate it either way?"

"Of course, it is." the deity walked slowly around the machine, "Mortals. Always meddling with things that they know nothing about. Now you want *me* to clean up *your* mess. Does your hubris know no bounds?"

As the God stepped up next to the General, the hole vibrated slightly and glowed crimson. The General immediately backed away, drawing his sidearm.

"What are you doing, Sergei?" The God inquired.

"Something is about to spill through again," Sergei answered as he motioned to the troops for assistance. The door opened as several small crimson creatures dropped down to the floor. Each one looked similar, thick skin with sickly green veins coursing throughout their miniature forms, claws that dripped a strange substance and they gave off the odor of sulfur.

The military teams stormed in, weapons drawn, ready to defend the General and the facility. The creatures growled as they aggressively marched forward, but froze in place when they saw the celestial being. Each creature cowered, dropping to the cold floor, not daring to meet his eyes.

The humans kept their weapons aimed at the diminutive creatures, awaiting the order from the General, who stood silently observing. The deity pointed to the hole and coldly muttered, "Leave *now*. Don't make me say it *again*."

Each one quietly and quickly jumped back into the hole in the air with no fuss. The God turned to the stunned humans and shrugged, "Demons. Always butting in when they aren't wanted."

"How," Sergei struggling to ask as his cigar fell to the floor, "how did you do that? Those things are *demons*?"

"Yes. Minor demons, but demons non the less."

"Why did they obey you?" The General asked suspiciously.

The deity looked at the men as they lowered their weapons and announced calmly with a mischievous smile, "It's classified."

"Answer me, villain!" Sergei pressed as he boldly stormed up to the deity, "Why would demons listen to you, unless you are in league with them? Is this a ruse on your part?"

"It's called respect, maybe you've heard of it before?" The God snapped, "They know who I am and what I am capable of doing. They fled because I told them to. I could have let them slaughter all of you."

"But you're powerless, they would've attacked you too. Surely they could tell somehow." Sergei countered.

The deity grinned, "They knew and yet they *still* obeyed. That is called respect and power. Something *you* might do well to learn."

"Begging my pardon, General," a soldier spoke up, "Can't we leave this thing imprisoned here? If it can deter other monsters from coming through, why not chain it to the wall here."

The God's gaze locked with the soldier's eyes, forcing him to freeze in place, "You can do that, but remember that I told the demons to leave. What makes you think that I *will* do again?"

"Everyone out!" The General barked.

The soldiers left in unison, except for the one that spoke. As Sergei picked his cigar up, he noticed that the soldier had a vacant gaze, as if in a trance. *Was the God causing this,* Sergei wondered, *Is it truly powerless?* The General walked up to the soldier and slapped his face as he ordered, "I gave you an order, soldier! I expect you to follow it. Now leave!"

The jolt caused the man to break his gaze from the God. He stuttered as he backed out of the room, rubbing his cheek, "Y-Yes s-sir. S-Sorry General."

Sergei turned his attention back to the deity as the door closed and eyed him before asking, "Can you close the hole or not?"

"Why should I? Something like *this* isn't done for free and magic *always* comes with a price, General."

"Stop playing games with me, monster!" The General demanded, which caused the God to chuckle, "What's so damn funny!"

"You are, General. You still view me in your military perspective as a human foe. An enemy. A terrorist, as you say. I'm above your *human* laws and none of these views you hold dear doesn't apply to me. I could simply step through the tear and be gone, if I wish, but I haven't."

"And why haven't you," Sergei eyes widened as he pointed his pistol at the deity as realization hit him that he had given his prisoner a means to escape.

"You people summoned me here, remember? If roles were reversed, wouldn't *you* demand compensation, especially when you didn't want to do it in the first place?"

"Name your price, then," Sergei lowered his weapon, but didn't holster it, "What will it take for you to assist us here?"

"Remove the shackles and we can talk," the deity held his arms out, rattling the chain.

"Out of the question, you will-"

"Will what? Flee? By now you know if I wanted to go, I would have done so. I need them off so I can close the rift and help with whatever trivial matters you need assistance with."

"What guarantee is there that you won't kill everyone here?"

"None. It's called faith for a reason, but do recall that it was *you* that brought me here. The choice is yours, Sergei."

The General muddled over the idea of freeing the God. He still didn't trust it fully so he tried another tactic, something he hated: a compromise.

"I will free you, so you can close the hole, then these go back in place. You close that, then we go upstairs and discuss the second job, as well as payment for your services."

The God thought for a moment, then coldly answered with a smile, "Agreeable."

Chapter Three

Wearily, the General unclipped a set of keys from a belt loop. He approached the deity as if He were a venomous viper, posed to strike. He unlocked the shackles as he nervously chewed on his extinguished cigar. Once the shackles came off, the God looked over his shoulder as he rubbed his wrists. A moment later, the hole was gone.

"How did you do that so quickly?"

"It's easy when you have the knowledge, something you mortals lack at this time," the deity answered as he held out his arms, "Shackles, please."

Sergei snapped the shackles back on as quickly as possible, wondering if the God was merely toying with him. As swiftly as it took for it to close the rift, the General considered that the God may not be as helpless as it let on.

"Where to, Sergei?"

"Follow me, please," the General opened the door and held it open for his prisoner. The guards looked on in awe as they snapped to attention. The General noticed their reaction and commanded, "At ease, men. You may disperse from hole duty. Our *friend* here took care of that little problem."

Sighs of relief and cheers erupted, several men brazenly patted the God on his back as the duo walked towards the stairwell. Sergei pulled his radio off his belt and ordered, "The hole is gone. Have the government officials meet us in the Section Three main lab."

"Sir, yes sir!"

The ascent up the stairs was quiet, with the exception of the jubilant soldiers. Sergei unlocked the door and held it for the deity. He directed them to a small hallway to the right that led to several elevators. Sergei pressed the button for the door to open. He looked over at the celestial being, noticing that he had a vacate look upon his perfect visage.

"Something wrong?" The General asked as the elevator dinged and the metal door slid open. The deity didn't reply but proceeded to enter the elevator of his own accord with Sergei followed closely behind. He hit the button for the third floor and asked as the door grinded closed, "You're awful quiet. What are you plotting?"

"It's classified," the God smirked, seeing the ire in the General's eye roll.

"I thought we agreed to not say that anymore."

"You did," the deity corrected, "I never agreed that *I* couldn't say it."

"So, you *are* plotting, aren't you?"

The God smiled, "Wouldn't *you* be?"

The General grumbled to himself as he lit his cigar once more just as the elevator dinged. The door opened up and the duo briskly walked down the corridor. It was much cleaner in appearance, unlike the rest of the facility, and everything shined. The floor was covered in white tiles and both the walls and ceiling were circular like an egg, seamlessly melding together as one.

Voices could be heard as they approached a black door with two soldiers on either side of it. The men saluted the General as they opened the door for him to enter. He quickly saluted back as the people inside argued between each other. The room grew silent as they noticed the deity smiling, unnerving everyone.

"Everyone, this is," Sergei pulled out the paper from his pocket as he announced, "Babalú-Ayé. He has graciously offered to help us with-"

"That doesn't look like a God," Johnson sneered in disgust, "This man is *not* God!"

"What do you mean by, oh," the deity chuckled, "you are one of *those* humans that's diluted himself into the rumors that there's only one God."

"It's not rumors, it's the truth!"

"Johnson, *your* God does exist, unfortunately."

"What do you mean by 'unfortunately'?"

"It means that He has many worshipers that do more harm than good in His name. You humans have done so many terrible deeds, hiding behind Him, using His name as a shield for your righteous hatred, bigotry, atrocities, and many genocides that He's isolated away from your kind in pain."

"God is all powerful, he can't feel pain that you speak of," Johnson snarled, "He is the one and only God who created everything. You know not what you speak of."

"Actually, I do because I've met Him. He's in pain because of His poorly written guidelines He handed down has been twisted by Man. He simply could fix it and end His needless suffering, but He's a prideful one. Now He waits for people like you to go before Him to be judged. Needlessly to say, not many get into His paradise."

"Blasphemous heathen!" enraged, Johnson rushed forward and punched the deity in the face. The sound of bones cracking echoed in the room as Johnson dropped down to his knees, wailing in pain. The deity, unfazed by the blow, turned his attention to the General and asked, "Is this worm my next task or is it something else?"

"No, but our problem is one of the human kind."

"When isn't this world's problems related to humanity?" The deity sighed, "It's not like you're going around tearing holes in the veil, right?"

"Babalú-Ayé, if you would please sit and listen to our proposal, I'm sure we can come up with a reasonable price for your help."

The deity observed the room and noticed something was missing, or rather, someone. As the God sat down, he stated, "Very well, but we aren't all present and accounted for at this meeting."

One of the government officials answered, "All are present and accounted for, sir. Now-"

"If that's true, then where's the little witchling at?"

"*She's* not a part of this equation."

"Then you're wasting my time." The deity sneered as he folded his arms across his chest. The men looked questioning at each other. Sergei grumbled, "She's not been read in and doesn't have the clearance for what we are going to discuss this evening."

"I don't care about *your* protocols; you *will* be making quite a few concessions or I walk. It's non-negotiable."

The General pointed at one of the guards, "Marcus, escort Ms. Binks to the meeting."

"While we wait," Sergei motioned to several men in white coats, "I'd like to introduce you to our weapons architects. Dr. Kon and Dr. Tivor."

The deity nodded slightly, but kept watching the door. The General wondered what the celestial being had up its ancient sleeves for her. What role would she have in all this, other than Jasmine summoning the deity?

"Hello, holy one." Dr Kon nodded, but felt uncomfortable when the God laughed.

"I'm far down the scales to be remotely considered a holy one," the deity's laughter muted as the witch entered the room meekly. With a kick of his foot, the God pushed the chair to his right and commanded, "Sit here, witchling."

Jasmine walked over, eyeing the General for permission. Sergei glared as he nodded, sucking more on his cigar which spoke to his level of anger and frustration. The deity gently patted the leather chair seat as the woman neared it.

"I don't bite," the celestial being grinned coyly as Jasmine sat down, "much...unless you ask nicely."

Jasmine blushed slightly as Sergei motioned for the scientists to begin. Dr. Tivor brought up a slideshow of different stats and graphs as Dr. Kon spoke, "As all of you may or may not know, our world is showing the signs of overpopulation. The coming decades we will have the issue of more people than food and resources, something we can't have. Our governments have come to the conclusion that we need a long-term solution to this crisis. One solution is mandatory sterilization for a select population, but this isn't a viable avenue to explore. Despite the breakthroughs in genetically modified foods, the demand will be too overwhelming globally."

"What do you want to do then?" The deity asked, showing little emotional changes.

"Our collective governments have agreed that we need to cull the population with viral outbreaks every five to ten years. Our target groups will be the elderly, the poor and underprivileged, and the chronically sick. As this population is reduced, this will free up resources and give a great financial boost for the majority of corporate parties involved in this endeavor."

Jasmine gasped as the men nodded, "Global genocide! You can't be seriously considering this?"

"That's the gist of it. People have to be sacrificed for humanity to live." Dr. Tivor said matter of fact, unfazed by Jasmine's outrage, "It's the best and most viable option we have."

"I can't be a part of this!" Jasmine stood up and slapped her hands on the table, "You can count me out!"

"You're already involved with all the summoning work you've been doing for us. This is what you signed up for."

"No one mentioned mass murder when I was recruited into this madness!"

"And yet you keep cashing those government checks as soon as they arrive. You're just as deep in this as the rest of us in this room. You can thank your new *friend* there. He's the only reason that you know this much classified information." The General interjected.

"I'm done with this place," Jasmine pushed her chair out and marched toward the exit.

"You can't leave, not after what you just heard," Sergei threatened as he motioned for the guards at the door to block her, "You're staying or leaving in a body bag, your choice witch!"

Sergei towered over the woman, smoke billowing from his cigar. He roughly grabbed her by the arm and forced her to sit back down.

"Get up again and I will personally shoot you myself!"

"No, you won't, General." The deity replied, his gaze froze the military officer in his tracks, "You touch her one more time or threaten her in any way. *I* will end your existence."

Jasmine felt a chilling hand gently grasp her hand. She could feel the raw power coursing inside the deity and wondered if the shackles were useless. Mentally she heard his voice once more,

"I mean it. You will not come to any harm as long as you stay by my side. You are nothing to them but a disposable tool, but to me, you're going to be a catalyst."

"I don't want anything to do with any of this. Just kill me swiftly, since I don't want to do as you command. I'm just a witch, nothing else."

"You can be much more than that, Jasmine. Never think otherwise or you will always be a rug for feet to be wiped on. You will be my catalyst, whether you like it or not. Don't take it as a threat, but know that I'm including you."

"I don't understand. Am I to be sacrificed for your part in this terrible deed?"

"*No child, but you are instrumental in saving the lives that would be arbitrarily extinguished by the plans of these governments.*"

"*You know what they are planning on doing,*" Jasmine gasped out loud, which garnered more glares, "*How?*"

The giggle in her head scared her more than the knowledge she gained tonight, "*I can see into the minds of men. I have a plan that I have to implement, but you humans have given me an opportunity that I couldn't pass up. The global cleansing will occur, but not how they will envision it.*"

As the presentation came to a close, the General looked over at the deity and asked, "You've been quiet through all this. What are your thoughts? Will you aid in this project?"

"I believe that your argument is a compelling one, full of logic. I suspect that you want me to tweak your viruses so it will do what your respected governments wish for them to do?"

"An astute observation, yes." Dr. Kon replied with a smile as he nodded to Dr. Tivor, who left the room to retrieve samples of the viruses, "Will you have to physically handle them for this to work?"

"Once these are removed," the deity dramatically rattled the shackle chain, "it will be done before you know it, but I require the witchling as an assistant, as well as all the blood samples from *all* the entities that reside here."

"Why?" Sergei blurted out.

"That's my price for my help," the deity declared coldly, "and the why? It's classified, General."

"Will you require my blood?" Jasmine asked as she bit her quivering bottom lip.

"Blood magic," Johnson shrieked as he clutched his hand, "Devil's work! You people are *all* damned!"

The General unlocked the wrist shackles and the deity snapped his finger, breaking Johnson's neck. Johnson's body collapsed in a heap; his head lay at an odd angle. The room went quiet, the General questioned mentally if he should slap the shackles back on the creature.

"Drama queen," the God muttered.

"Why did you murder Johnson?" Dr. Kon asked as he covered his mouth in horror.

"Seriously?" The celestial being incredulously replied, "You people are talking about global genocide and you're going to get bent out of shape over one death? Humanity's hypocrisy knows no bounds. Now be a good little human and get those blood samples for me, *now*."

Dr. Kon rushed out of the room, gagging as the contents of his stomach churned. The deity stood up and walked over to Johnson's corpse. He kneeled down and placed a hand on his limp body and smiled, "He's now with his God and it's not going well for him."

"You're not Babalú-Ayé, are you?" Jasmine mentally asked, fearing that she knew the truth.

The deity looked at her and winked as he stood up. Dr. Tivor walked in the room, nearly dropping the viruses upon seeing the body.

48

The scientist gulped as he shakily sat the safe box on the table. Dr. Kon swiftly followed with a large collection of vials of different colors of blood.

The scientists backed away as the deity moved forward. Jasmine wanted to follow the men but she couldn't move. She wasn't sure if it was from fear or if the God was holding her in place. The deity beckoned the witch to him, her body moved forward.

"Do you trust me, Jasmine?"

She hugged the celestial being as tears trickled down her face, *"I don't know. What are you going to do to me?"*

"Good answer, you shouldn't. I plan on being intimate with you."

"You mean rape, don't you?"

"No," the deity looked concerned at the woman, *"it will be intimate magically. It's the only way you can save lives. Do you understand what I'm asking of you?"*

"Sex magic, without the actual physical act."

"You almost sound hurt. Would you rather it be physical?"

Jasmine shrugged, *"I don't have a say in the matter. It's not like I could fight you off, not when you were never powerless this whole time."*

"You always have a choice, witchling." The God placed two fingers under the woman's chin and gently moved her head up to look at him, *"I told you that I would never hurt you and I meant it. You're the key to saving many people with this rite. I can tell that you don't want so many people to die, which is why it has to be you. Your part is the protection."*

The General marched over to the God and demanded, "If you're done cuddling with the conjurer, get on with your part. These samples can't be unsupervised for long."

The deity glanced at Sergei as more smoke bellowed in its face. He waved a hand over the both boxes as he continued to hold Jasmine.

"How do we do this?" Jasmine asked mentally.

"*Grant me your energy freely and we will mingle together, weaving a potent protection into the viruses.*"

"*It's embarrassing to say but I want you to take me physically. I want to feel you inside me.*"

"*If we do this,*" the deity warned, "*your physical form may die.*"

"*I'm not of any consequence to anyone. If I die, it will be for a good cause. I freely offer my body and magical energy to you but...what's your name?*"

"*I'm known as Harbinger, the destroyer of worlds, protector, creator of life, bringer of death and resurrection...*"

Harbinger took control over everyone in the room and forced them to chant in an unknown language as they formed a protective circle around the two. Jasmine laid back on the table, and allowed the ancient God to enter her body. Powerful energy swirled around the two and slowly directed into the viruses.

"Please, Harbinger!" The witch pleaded, "Take me, now!"

"No," the ancient God replied, "You will die if I do. You are on the brink of death from all that you're giving right now."

"Let me die. Give me a blissful death and peace." Jasmine weakly muttered as she slipped in and out of consciousness.

Harbinger grunted as he whispered in her ear, "Your time isn't done. You have much to do and little time to accomplish it."

The witch gasped as she felt the ancient God enter her core. Her eyes rolled back in her head as she involuntarily chanted the same strange language spoken by the men. Jasmine felt herself leaving her body. She observed what was happening in the room and noticed that the deity saw her as he mounted her still form.

"Do you want to return or join me?"

Confused, the witch replied, *"What do you mean? I'm already dead. What else can I do?"*

Harbinger stood up and stated, *"It's a simple question. Return to your body and feel all the pain involved with what we just performed or follow me and I will guide you to your true path."*

"Why give me a choice? I told you that I wanted to die like this. Why keep asking and what do mean by my true path?"

"Because you always have a choice, so choose, witchling and discover that for yourself..."

Chapter Four

Present day

Meg opened the refrigerator door for the third time in less than five minutes. Nothing looked appetizing; more condiments and less food to use them on. She sighed loudly as she threw her head back, staring at the ceiling as if it would open a portal that held a cornucopia of delicious foods. It didn't happen.

I'm a witch, I should be able to make that happen.

Meg closed the door in disgust as the prospect of what she had to do loomed over her, like a dark cloud of negativity.

Ugh, I got to go to the grocery store.

Meg trudged out of the kitchen, feeling dejected. It wasn't that the witch didn't like shopping, it had more to do with dealing with people. It drained her mentally, physically, and emotionally because of Meg's empathic nature.

The witch tended to absorb other people's emotions, both good and bad, like a sponge, whether she wanted to or not. This took a heavy toll on her body as well, which meant she had to perform personal cleansings every so often or the witch's health declined.

Lately, Meg has been having to cleanse more often than what she was used to doing, which was a cause for concern. She knew that something was happening but the answer eluded her. The witch walked through the living room to rummage through the massive pile of clothes in the laundry basket.

Meg lived the single life in her three-bedroom country house in the suburbs of Portland, but currently was having some physical fun with her next-door neighbor Joe. She managed to purchase her house before the great housing boom happened; when prices of properties, whether rental or for sale, skyrocketed.

Meg thanks the Gods and Goddesses for what she had because many were forced into the streets because of the greed of landlords and their property management teams. With the influx of travelers looking to settle down in

Oregon, the supply of rentals couldn't meet the demand, so prices soared.

The witch slipped off her nightgown and let it pool around her feet. She grabbed black sweatpants and a teal Cami top. *It was just a run to the grocery store, might as well be comfortable,* Meg thought as she sat down on the plush red couch to put her sneakers on.

A black blur of movement from the corner of her eye caught her attention. The witch saw the same ghost hanging out by her bamboo plants, vacantly gazing at her.

Meg stood up, placing her hands on her cocked hips, and snarked, "Do you have anything new to say today, ghost boy?"

The ghost rasped, "*Prepare, the Reset is coming...*"

"Good to know, but what does that even mean?"

"*Prepare, the Reset is coming...*"

"Yep, just as I thought," Meg grumbled, "Same warning, different day. Would it be possible for a little more information than that?"

"Prepare, the Reset is coming..." The ethereal form repeated.

"You're so helpful. Wait, here's a thought: why don't *you* prepare for the Reset since it's so important to you?"

The ghost hoovered there silently for a moment before uttering, *"Prepare, the Reset is coming..."*

The witch threw her hands up in the air in frustration, "Useless ghost!"

"Prepare, the Reset is coming..."

Meg wadded up a pair of socks and threw them at the ghost's face, "Put a sock in it, you century old broken record!"

She grabbed her cellphone and her clutch purse, glaring at her infuriating house guest as she walked out the door. She could hear its muffled voice repeat the same phrase.

This "interaction" between the witch and the ghost had gone on like this for several months and every day it said that same phrase, no variation. It was like talking to a voice-activated recorded message and as interesting as watching moss grow on a tree. Meg walked off her porch and with her fob, unlocked her Mazda CX-5.

She turned the ignition on and clutched the steering wheel with her eyes closed. She took several deep breaths, calming down and said to herself, "Not a great way to start this trip."

As she put her SUV in reverse, the radio announcer droned on about the latest influenza outbreak, which seemed to be the favorite topic of late. Meg groaned mentally as she drove down the street,

It's just the flu, what's the big deal?

The news was on every station, both TV and the radio, giving warning about how terrible this flu season is; advising citizens to practice good hand washing habits as well as social distancing.

The newscaster announced, "*In relation to this flu pandemic. People have been reported to having hallucinations, like seeing things and hearing strange voices. Experts can only speculate that it could be related to a higher than normal fever with this strain of the flu, but not enough research has been done to substantiate this. Hospital officials have claimed that people have also been showing some erratic behavior to the point of being detrimental to themselves and those around them. 'It's as if they have no concept of self-preservation,' one ER doctor was quoted at yesterday's World Health Organization conference."*

Meg wondered what the point was when people don't do these things in the first place, at other times during the year. The witch clutched the steering wheel bitterly as she came to a stoplight, dreading having to deal with the people at the grocery store. Humans tended to panic buy during moments of bad weather, but it got worse during the flu season.

Traffic was surprisingly light, considering that it was three in the afternoon. Normally the main streets in Portland would be packed with people trying to get to and from work, crazy lane jumpers, and pedestrians crossing the road anywhere but the crosswalks. The radio announcer talked about the president, stating, "*In other news, today the president decided to close the nation's last remaining submarine base at Groton, Connecticut during the pandemic. When asked why he made this odd decision, the president dismissively responded by say, 'Those funny little black keep sinking anyway!'*"

Meg rolled her eyes as she glanced around, wondering if there was some event happening elsewhere. It wasn't time for the World Naked Bike Ride or the Adult Box Derby. Maybe a concert downtown? Whatever it was, the witch hoped that the grocery store would be just as barren of foot traffic.

Meg drove several more miles down the road. The announcer talked more about the latest influenza virus and its effects on the population, which Meg promptly turned off the radio. When she got in view of the big box chain superstore, the witch grinded her teeth, seeing it's parking lot was packed.

Is this where everyone decided to go today?

People were ambling about, like they had nothing better to do and nowhere to be, which made it difficult for Meg to hunt for a parking spot, lest she run over someone. She meandered up and down the lanes, getting more frustrated with each passing moment. A glimmer of hope shined as she caught sight of a place to park, but it was occupied as she got closer. Meg beeped her horn at a young lady that merely stood in the open parking spot.

No response.

The young lady was dressed in sleek black yoga pants with a blue sports bra on, and had an MP3 player strapped to her left arm but the earbuds daggled freely. Meg held her hand on the horn and let it blare for a good ten seconds, hoping that the woman would move.

Nothing.

Meg rolled her window and shouted, "Move it, lady! This isn't a Starbucks for you to hang out at, you know. Other people want to use *that* spot!"

The woman looked at the witch with a vacant stare and asked in a melancholy voice, "Will you please hit the gas and run me over?"

Perplexed, Meg replied, "What? No, I won't do that! Why would you even ask that?"

"Because you have a car and the means to do it," the woman coldly answered.

"Go play in the street if you want that sort of action," Meg snarled, tiring of the woman's games, "If you want to die, that's your best bet. Not here!"

The young lady's voice sent a chill down Meg's spine, "Thanks for help. I will go and find my last ride."

Meg watched as the lady walked. She wore no shoes and the soles of her feet appeared blistered and a harsh shade of red. The young lady hobbled her way towards 82nd Ave, her face devoid of all emotion. Meg eased her SUV into the parking spot, keeping an eye on the strange lady. Worry seeped into her mind.

"Did I just tell that girl to kill herself?" Meg spoke aloud. She rolled up her window and got out. As the witch walked purposefully towards the store, she kept looking back over her shoulder. She didn't see the depressed lady. Part of her wished that she could, the guilt ate away at her.

As Meg entered the store, an overwhelming sense of dread and despair hit her like a freight train, knocking her to her knees. She gasped as she clutched her chest, trying to make sense of what just occurred. Meg gained her composure as she stood up and walked over and grabbed a shopping cart. The people within the store all had the same vacant stare that the jogger had outside.

It was both unsettling and unnerving, but the witch needed groceries. She kept her head down as she maneuvered her way down the congested aisles, snatching what food she could get. The odd thing Meg noticed was that the shelves were full and abundant, the people were wandering around like zombies in cheap B-movies with little interest in anything.

Even the store clerks seemed like they were injected with an overdose of apathy. Meg's journey deeper into the store got stranger, if that was possible. She overheard a conversation between two men that gave her pause.

"Do you know how to get out of here?"

"That's what I'm looking for, a way out. I think the knives are the next aisle over."

"A gun." The first man replied, his voice oozing of melancholy, "A gun will make the best exit."

A store clerk overheard their conversation as he stepped up beside them and flatly stated, "The guns are this way. I have the key to unlock the cabinet. We can take turns exiting. Follow me..."

In unison, the three men walked away towards the sporting goods section. Meg's jaw dropped.

What the hell is going on!?!

A woman over in the next aisle ripped off a metal merchandise hook. Meg watched on in horror as she slowly but forcefully pressed the hook into her neck, piercing her carotid artery. Blood drained out like a little crimson river as the lady dropped down to the floor, bleeding out with a smile.

No matter where she went, people all around her were finding different things to end their lives. A teenage boy, no more than fourteen, dove off the top of a ceiling bike rack, head first on the floor. The crackling of his neck was etched into the witch's memory forever.

"What the fuck is wrong with you people!?!" Meg shouted with her hands on the side of her head, but no one seem to notice, let alone acknowledge her, except for one person. A woman's violet eyes caught the witch's full attention as they seemed to pulsate. Meg had a sense of dread as this female watched her, like an eagle ready to snatch an unsuspecting field mouse.

The woman was wearing a tattered black robe that ran the length of her form, pooling at her feet. The mysterious woman smiled as she looked towards the sporting goods section as gunshots echoed throughout the store. The sound had people turning their heads as they ambulated in that direction.

Meg ran as fast as she could, knocking any food she could reach into her cart. It seemed like everywhere she went, the mysterious lady was nearby, watching her.

As she rounded the corner to go to the check-outs, Meg watched more people killing themselves. One woman sat in a forklift with a heavy pallet of shrink-wrapped bleach boxes hoisted in the air. The woman climbed out of cab, stood under the forks, and pulled on a piece of rope that was attached to the lift lever. The forklift load dropped down as the woman laid on the floor, crushing most of her upper body.

A manager walked over to the forklift and pulled up on the lever, raising the load up as Meg got to him and screeched, "Hurry up, she might not make it! Why didn't you stop her?"

The manager turned to Meg and asked, his eyes vacant as everyone else in the store, "I didn't know what she was doing until now," He held out the sticky, crimson rope and asked, "Would you like to exit next or can I go before you? We can share."

Meg slapped the employee hard, "Hell no, I don't want to kill myself! Why is any of this happening?"

"I'm not killing myself," the manager corrected the witch, "I'm exiting this place. There's a big difference. Now if you'll excuse me, I must go..."

"In that case," Meg snarked as she held her hand out, "give me your store keys so I can rob this place easier when I come back tonight."

The manager reached into his vest pocket and retrieved the store keys. He dropped them into an astonished Meg's hand and said, "Take them. Take everything. There're more security keys in the front office so take them too. I really have to exit now."

Meg stumbled backwards and turned as she heard the forklift load lower down once more. She sprinted to what she assumed was the front office. It was a small hallway that had several offices on each side. Meg peered in the first room and saw several employees had killed themselves, their bodies lying on the tile floor. One with a pen in his neck and the other had stuck a knife into an outlet.

She cautiously stepped over the dead bodies and reached for a metal box on the far wall. She yanked on the handle but it didn't open. Meg groaned as she spent several frustrating minutes trying to find the right key that the former manager gifted to her.

With a click, the box opened, revealing a row of keys, each one labeled for convenience. She grabbed them all and shoved them into her pockets. She left the office and found the door that said *"money office"* stenciled in green paint.

Why not take a little money to go?

As she entered the room, a young man looked at her, his eyes vacant, and asked, "Are you here to help me find the exit?"

"It all depends on you, kiddo. I do possess the knowledge that you seek, but it comes at a cost." Meg dramatically stated, trying to hide the fact that this young man, who might have been twenty, wanted to die like everyone else did.

He beamed a raptured smile, "Name it. What does my heavenly angel want from me?"

Heavenly angel? Meg had to restrain a burst of giggles. She had never been called that before, let alone anything else sweet and corny. She watched him closely as he dropped down onto his knees, smiling mindlessly up at her. It was a shame that this stud was going to go to waste. She thought about taking him home with her, but knowing her luck, the kid would die messy, leaving her to clean it up.

The witch pointed at the black locker and asked, "Is the money safe inside that? If yes, can you open it?"

"I need a key. Or I can bash at the doors with my head until it opens up for you. I'd do anything for you, my angel..."

"Erm," Meg stammered slightly, feeling uncomfortable as she showed the kid the manager's key set, "Is it one of these?"

"It will have a label with the word *'money box'* attached to it."

Meg reached into her pockets and fumbled a bunch onto the floor. The young man picked them all up for her and held one aloft proudly, "This is what you seek. Will you grant me my exit?"

Meg pushed past him, her eyes stinging with tears, nothing that she could do would persuade him from ending his life so she blurted out, half choking on her sobs, "Go back out on the floor. There's plenty of exits to choose from. Find one and leave me alone now, please."

The young man stood up and hugged Meg from behind, causing her guilt to worsen.

"Thanks, my sweet angel. I'll never forget your kindness and generosity..."

Meg gulped as she squeezed her eyes tightly together. Tears escaped as she asked, "What's your name, kid?"

"Trevor. Trevor Kline, my angel. Farewell and may we meet again in your heavenly home..." He let go and walked silently out of the money office.

Chapter Five

Meg stood there in silence as her emotions became too much for her to handle. The witch repeatedly hit the panel covered wall as she cried out in anger and frustration, "Why? Why Trevor, damnit? The fuck did he do to deserve such a terrible fate? It's not right, nor is it fair!"

She frustratedly growled as she turned and slid down the wall, putting her head onto her knees. Meg didn't know what to make of this day. Everyone was intent on killing themselves. Something was amiss, this much the witch knew, but wasn't sure exactly what? Was this a new bioengineered weapon, causing people to lose all traces of self-preservation?

Am I living in an M Night Shyamalan movie?

Meg shook her head as she bitterly laughed at the thought of Mother Nature killing off humanity. *It's not like we don't deserve it with all we've done to Her.* Unlike the movie, the people in the store shouldn't have been affected because there's no plant life in here, with the exception of the garden section, but it was isolated outside.

Meg stood up and unlocked the black cabinet. Rows of blue money bags sat across the shelves, each one had numbers on them corresponding to a specific department. At the bottom of the cabinet, Meg found a decent size reusable cloth sack. She grabbed it and loaded it down with all the contents of the safe. The bag sagged heavily as the witch slung it over her shoulder and walked out. Meg pondered exploring the other offices, but didn't want to run into another Trevor.

The witch rushed over to her shopping cart and paused when she heard a familiar voice high above her head. Her eyes bulged when she saw Trevor standing precariously on the top safety rail of a thirty-foot-tall Tri-Arch stocking ladder. The kid's vacant eyes fell on Meg as he wobbled with his arms extended, "Watch me fly, my angel..."

"No!" The witch screamed as she held her hand out, wishing that she could somehow stop him. He smiled at her, all the way down, as his neck snapped audibly. His body twisted, making it appear that he was decapitated from her point of view.

Meg rushed over to one of the checkout stands and emptied the contents of her stomach in a little black trash can. The witch spat more bile out and became unnerved by the stillness of the store. She saw people killing themselves and yet, they never made a sound, as though they weren't in pain. She hurried over and grabbed her shopping cart and rushed to the exit.

Meg paused at the automatic doors as a strong soapy floral odor enveloped her senses. *Jasmine?* She could tell that someone else was with her, trying to get her attention. The witch gulped as she slowly turned around and was met by the mysterious lady.

The woman watched her as her violet eyes pulsated. Meg tensed as the woman reached out and caressed her cheek, like a lover would do.

"Are..." Meg stammered, "Are you the one causing all of this?"

"My role in this is to keep you safe from those that wish you harm."

"Why me?" Meg demanded as she pointed over at the ladder, "Why wouldn't you protect Trevor? What did he do wrong? Why am I worth more than his life?"

"He died because he had to. We can't save everyone from this, only those chosen to bear witness to these events."

"What the fuck does that even mean?" Meg growled, feeling frustrated by this woman's cryptic talk. "Answer me! No more games!"

The mysterious lady smiled, causing the witch to lose some of her resolve, "You're not ready to comprehend this yet. You need to leave and be prepared. Others have the knowledge that you seek, if you ask the right questions. I'm forbidden to say anything at this time, but know that I'm neither friend or foe, witch."

The mysterious lady turned and sauntered off and then vanished.

Stunned, Meg could only stand there like a fool, gaping at what just happened while questioning her own sanity. She turned and sprinted out the door, passing an employee who stated, "Come back. Or not, I don't care..."

She fumbled around in her pocket and retrieved her Fob to unlock her vehicle. She tossed her hoard of groceries haphazardly into the trunk and then shoved the cart out her way, not caring where it went. She slammed the hatch closed and then slipped in behind the wheel. Meg tossed the bag of money on the passenger seat as she ignited the engine.

Panic gripped her heart as she peeled out of the parking lot. As she got on the road, the scene had taken a complete one-eighty turn for the worse. Vehicles were everywhere, some driving while others sat in place, idling. People were ambling about, like zombies in a horror movie.

One side of the road, Meg witnessed an elderly man standing in front of a metal barrel as flames peaked out of the top. Much to her chagrin, the man crawled into the barrel and let the flames engulf his body with a blissful smile. Meg turned on the radio, hoping music could distract her.

The radio announcement kept repeating itself, which caught her by surprise. It wasn't the usual emergency broadcast message nor was it coming from an official government speaker trying to placate the masses. It was the same statement, monotonously uttered with the same enthusiasm as many of the people she ran into at the store.

"The Reset is now upon you...Exit well..."

Meg swerved around the congestion of cars and people, wanting to go home and barricade herself inside and let this pass. When her home came into her thoughts, so did the ghost.

That broken record has some explaining to do when I get home, the witch thought as she pressed harder on the accelerator. The witch slowed her SUV down as she finally saw the suicidal jogger. The woman had been stripped of her clothes and tied to a signal light post. A group of four, two men and two women, took turns cutting on her or punching her body.

The worst part was that the jogger kept smiling.

One man straddled his hips between her thighs as Meg's breaks squealed. He turned and pointed at the witch and calmly commanded, "She's next. Bring her flesh here."

The group marched towards Meg's SUV as the man with the jogger sank his teeth into her chest, ripping a chunk out and turning his gaze back on Meg. The witch pressed hard on the accelerator as one of the women jumped up on the hood. The female looked wrong, her eyes were wild and feral. The sclera was no longer white, it had been consumed with an inky black substance.

The woman punched and clawed at the windshield, trying to get to the witch. Meg had a difficult time trying to see past her assailant, but she kept speeding up.

"Come, pretty one," the woman snapped her mouth as a foamy brown spittle dripped onto the windshield, "Feed me your lovely face!"

"Eat asphalt and choke, bitch!" Meg retorted as she slammed hard on the brakes. The woman howled as her body was violently tossed end over end. She bounced several times before coming to a complete stop, lying limp on the road. Meg eyed her as she tried catching her breath.

The wild woman lifted her head up, glaring at the witch. Parts of her face had been torn off from the impact, pieces of flesh dangled in spots. The woman didn't flinch as she peeled her skin off and slowly chewed it menacingly at Meg.

As the woman stood up, Meg turned her SUV down one of the side streets. She kept glancing at her rear-view mirror, expecting the crazy lady to be giving chase, like the T-1000 in *Terminator 2: Judgement Day*. She sped up when she finally saw the crazed female standing at the end of the road behind her, watching Meg speed away.

The witch turned the radio off, not wanting to hear the same message over and over any more. After several minutes of winding through the different neighborhoods,

Meg made it to her house. She put it in park and turned off the engine, she cautiously looked around for any signs of aggressive people. She stepped out of the SUV and ran over to the front door and unlocked it.

The neighborhood seemed quiet and unaffected by whatever was happening, but Meg had the feeling that it was just an illusion. It took her several trips to bring in all of the groceries, she was about to close and lock the front door when she remembered the money sack.

Meg rolled her eyes and cursed, "Fuck sake!"

She reached over and grabbed the aluminum bat that sat in the corner by the door and crept back outside. She walked with her back to her house so she could have a better chance of seeing any unwelcome visitors. The witch opened the passenger side door and grabbed the heavy bag and slung it over her shoulder. She was about to close the door when she felt a hand grab her ass.

Meg growled as she tried to swing her bat, but ended up striking the interior of her

SUV. The hand quickly let go and a male's voice spoke apologetically, "Whoa! Whoa! Whoa, Meg! It's just me, Joe. I didn't mean to upset you. I saw that you came home and -"

"And you wanted your thick skull cracked open like a cantaloupe? Sorry, I'm not in the mood to give you your exit. Find someone else to do it!"

Confused, Joe replied, "Exit? What are you talking about? I just thought I'd come over and hang out with my favorite little witch today since I have a few nights off."

"Oh," Meg replied as she closed and locked her SUV and rushed to get back in her house. Joe followed close behind and stated, "Oh? That's all I get from you? Can I get a better explanation as to why you're all of a sudden carrying a weapon outside?"

Meg rolled her eyes as she got to the front door. She turned and stuck the barrel end of the bat under Joe's chin, her jaw muscles twitching, "Sure, if it will shut you up!"

She noticed that he looked normal. He didn't have a vacant stare or the feral black eyes. Guilt stuck her once more so she added as her face softened, "Get inside. It's not safe out here."

Joe looked at her and then all around, feeling perplexed, "Safe from what?"

Meg opened the door with a huff, "In or out, Joe! Once I close this door, I'm not opening it for anyone or anything else, got it?"

"Right," Joe grunted as he pushed past Meg. She closed the door quickly and locked the deadbolt. Joe observed her as she peaked out the curtains every so often. She slung the money sack onto the couch as she plopped down beside it, feeling exhausted and drained.

Joe got on his knees and nestled his body between her legs. He gently massaged her thighs and asked, "Now that we're locked up in here, will you tell me who's chasing you?"

"I don't rightly know how to explain it. Frankly, I'm not sure what happened really did happen today." Meg replied with her eyes closed, her body shaking.

Joe stood up and picked up Meg's bag. He noted how heavy it was as he sat down with it in his lap and perused its contents. He carefully unzipped one of the blue bags and saw that it was overstuffed with money and rolls of coins.

"Did you rob a bank or something?"

Meg opened her eyes, confused by the question until she saw him holding her bag, "No, just that large superstore on 82nd Ave. I was being my snarky self and the manager gave me the keys. So, I cleaned them out and didn't have to pay for my groceries."

"You *robbed* the store?" Joe incredulously gasped, "No wonder you're being all paranoid, the cops are after you."

The witch bitterly laughed, "I wish it was that simple."

"So, explain it to me so I can understand, please? I'm worried about you."

Meg looked over at her bamboo plants and saw the ghost was swaying in and out of existence. She narrowed her eyes at the spectre as she barked, "Care to add to this conversation now that this Reset is happening, ghost boy?"

Joe observed that the ghost that had been residing here seemed different than it did before, it had more distinguishing features and more solid. "You think that its warning is happening now, Meg?"

The ghost moved away from its usual spot and spectre hovered in front of them, his eyes were more focused and alive.

"*You are correct...The Reset is happening now...*" The ghost uttered ethereally.

"Look who's no longer a broken record anymore!" Meg snarked as her irritation grew, "You could've thrown me a better bone about it these past few weeks!"

"*I wanted to, Meg, I truly did...*" The ghost lamented as it swayed back and forth, "*I was compelled to only say what I kept repeating...*"

"Are you able to talk freely about it now?" Joe asked as he put his arm around her shoulders. The ghost looked up at the ceiling. It was quiet for about a minute before it answered.

"I am allowed to talk, though I don't completely understand the Reset...I only know what I've been told, nothing more..."

Meg impatiently waved her hand to continue, but the spectre was silent.

"What the hell is the Reset, jackass!" Meg bit out through gritted teeth, her jaw muscles twitching.

"Calm down Meg," Joe softly spoke near her ear, "Remember that he's just now regained his freedom to speak."

"I don't care!" The witch snapped as she glared at her neighbor, "You haven't seen what I've seen today. I want answers, damnit!"

"I will tell you what I know, though I need to be asked...It's not by my doing that I'm like this..."

"Fine, what is the Reset?" Meg groaned in a huff as she crossed her arms across her chest.

"It is the extinguishing event of a civilization..."

Joe gasped, "Are you talking about the end of the world, like the apocalypse?"

The ghost thought for a moment and then cryptically replied, "*Yes...And no...*"

"I see that your vague side has returned," the witch snarked as she stood up. She walked over and grabbed a bottle of wine and a snack pack from one of her grocery bags, "Why do I get the feeling that this is going to be an exhausting explanation?"

"So, the world is changing, is that it," Joe inquired.

"*Yes...The Reset occurs when necessary change is needed for the Earth to heal...*"

"When was the last time this happened?" Meg asked as she drank straight from the bottle, "Why is there no record of it happening?"

"*It occurs when a civilization becomes too advanced technologically...A certain amount of balance is needed between it and nature...When a civilization skews too far from its connection with nature, change is needed to bring it back into balance...*"

"What civilizations did this happen to?" Joe pressed, feeling like he didn't want to hear the answer as unease filled his mind.

The ghost looked up at the ceiling for a couple of minutes, listening intently to a voice that neither of them could hear before replying, "*Names of most have been lost through the annals of time, but I'm told that you may know of Atlantis...Everything about it, including the vast expanse of land it stood on, was ripped from this world...*"

Meg spat wine from her mouth as she blurted out, "What! You're telling us that Atlantis was obliterated from the face of the Earth because they didn't live in harmony with nature? Is that going to happen to us?"

"*No, but it was one of the most extreme cases that the Reset had to take due to how technologically advanced they were...They were able to combat the change for a time, but in the end, it was decided that the entire continent had to be removed physically to another plane of existence...*"

"How is that even possible," Joe spoke as he thought about the incredible claim.

"The ones that monitor our world are not of our world...They watch humanity for the signs that they are becoming out of touch with nature...When it occurs, they set the Reset into motion…It's not an event that happens rapidly...It takes time so it not noticed by other less advanced civilizations...Atlantis left a wound on the Earth that has yet to heal and because of that, many strange and unexplainable events occur in that region..."

"When did this Reset start for us here in the U.S.?" Meg asked, but made sure to gulp down her drink this time.

"The Reset is not bound to this continent alone...This one is a global cleansing that's been in effect for several decades...Humanity has been systematically moved far from its connection to nature by way of Interglobal technology...People are more connected to each other and have lost their identity...There are several layers to this Reset, unlike other ones..."

"I can see how that can be considered a catalyst for the Reset, but why is everyone dying or going crazy?" The witch asked.

The ghost fixed its deadeye stare on her with a knowing look, sending a chill down her spine, as it cryptically answered, "*Ask the Protector...*"

"The Protector?" Joe stated as confusion racked his brain, "Who is this person?"

The ghost went silent.

"What is its role in all of this?" He demanded.

More silence.

"Let me guess," Meg spoke as she chugged more wine, "you're forbidden from talking about it?"

The ghost nodded with a sympathetic smile.

Joe stood up, feeling frustrated as he paced around the living room. He clenched his jaw muscles so tightly that they were noticeably twitching.

"How do we talk to it, the Protector?" He growled.

"You don't...She will talk to you only if and when you are ready...For now, be prepared to fight for your lives because if you don't, then you will become a casualty of the cleansing..."

Chapter Six

Outside, they could hear screaming. People were letting out wild shrieks, causing Meg to rigidly sit up. She snaked her body off the couch as Joe walked over to the window. He peered out the curtain to see what the commotion was all about.

One of the neighbors was being dragged out of their house by her hair towards a small group of people in the street. They proceeded to kick, stab, and bite her body until the woman went silent. Joe watched on in horror as other people came willingly outside and allowed the crazed thugs to do whatever they desired to them without a fight. It unnerved him seeing that his neighbors were all smiling, even as they were being assaulted.

"Get away from the fucking window before they see you!" The witch hissed.

Joe looked down at her, his face in complete shock, but as he turned to look outside, a face stared back at him. The man's visage was twisted with a bloody grin, pieces of flesh clung between his teeth. The man reared back and punched the window pane, shattering it, and dragged Joe outside.

Meg covered her mouth, stifling a scream as she scurried out of the room to her bedroom. She could hear her friend crying out in pain, but there was nothing that she could do for him. The witch dragged her bed mattress over to the door to use it as a barricade to buy herself time to think. She went over to the closet and grabbed out a small aluminum bat as more glass shattered.

The ghost appeared next to Meg and stated, "*They've breached your home...*"

"You think?" The witch sarcastically whispered, "Go see how many are in here!"

The ghost disappeared and all Meg could think about as she held her bat like a professional player was how to get to her SUV and make a run from the crazies. She could hear them stomping around, snarling noises echoed down the hallway. Things were being broken as the intruders searched the witch's house.

"There's four of them and they are coming this way...Joe is dead..."

Meg curtly nodded as she struggled to control her emotions. She hoped that her friend died quickly and didn't suffer, but she knew that these freaks would make it last. Picture frames were being knocked off the hallway walls, each one getting louder and meant that she was going to have to fight. She walked backwards, keeping an eye on the door, towards the window.

She saw more people running through her backyard in different directions, hunting for their next victim. Across the eight-foot-tall privacy fence, Meg could see several ropes swinging from the great oak tree next door. She knew that the occupants of that house had no children and never had tree swings before.

The witch had a feeling that she knew what, or rather who, was dangling from the ropes. Bangs on the bedroom door caused Meg to jump slightly. The door jostled open, enough for one of the thugs to see her.

"More food..." The wild-eyed man excitedly groaned as he pushed harder against the door. The mattress bucked several times before it yielded to the barrage, it bowed as it fell flat on the floor. The door was open slightly more but was kept from opening up all the way. The wild thugs all crammed their bodies into the opening, hoping to somehow squirm their way inside.

The witch seized the opportunity as she rushed over and repeatedly swung her bat down on the protruding heads. She growled frantically with each swing; her teeth clamped down as her survival rage showed itself.

Blood spattered her clothes with each blow. Meg leaned on the bat like a cane, trying to catch her breath from exertion. The bodies of the thugs stacked up on each other, motionless as blood trickled down their heads like a macabre water fountain.

The door jolted as the lithe form of a woman dove into the room, startling the witch. The new intruder fluidity moved to her feet like a feline. She eyed Meg hungrily as she snarled, "I'm going to eat you slowly. Your screaming will be legendary."

"If I had a nickel every time I heard something like that," the witch lifted the bat, "I'd be a rich witch."

The woman rushed at Meg with her arms outstretched. The witch swung her weapon, but the blow was blocked by the crazed woman's arms. She tackled Meg, causing her to lose her grip on the bat.

She pinned Meg's arms down under the weight of her body. The witch squirmed, trying to get free as the crazed woman leaned down and licked her from cheek to cheek slowly.

The woman gasped like a lover, "Your skin is so soft and tastes so sweet," she caressed Meg's side just under her shirt, "I bet your insides are even sweeter. I want to know..."

The woman pulled out a blood encrusted knife and held it over Meg's face. She glided it along her jawline as she leaned down and kissed her quivering lips as she whispered, "Don't worry, bitch. I will share with you. I don't want you to starve, like me."

"Why are you doing this?" Meg pleaded, trying to keep the crazed female preoccupied for a chance to escape.

"Why?" The woman got nose to nose with the witch, her face seemed more feral, "I'm starving and I want your sweet succulent meat. I want you in every way possible. I want to eat you, fuck you, be you because it's what I am now! Now hold still, I'm going to cut on you."

Meg flinched as she felt the cold steel of the woman's blade caress her side. She yelped as the sharp edge slit away at her skin, she bit her bottom lip to stifle a scream. The witch didn't want to alert other crazed people because her current situation could take a turn for the worse.

Before her, the woman triumphantly held a piece of skin in front of Meg's face, her own blood dripped onto her lips. The woman took a bite off it, savoring it as she slowly chewed. She grabbed the witch by her jaw and coldly commanded, "Open up. Your turn to eat."

"I'm not hungry," Meg weakly replied.

The woman slapped the witch several times, "Don't spurn my precious gift to you. Open your pretty mouth, *now*!"

Meg didn't want to look at her assailant, her cheeks stung from the hits. The crazed female dug her fingers into the wound, causing Meg to scream. She felt something sticky and wet drop into her croaking mouth.

"Chew it, bitch. I want to show you how delicious you taste."

Meg begrudgingly compiled, feeling nauseous at the knowledge of what she was eating.

"See?" The female cooed as she lovingly touched Meg's cheek, "That wasn't so bad. I told you that you're yummy. Why must you fight me?"

"Because," the witch decided to sway the perverse woman as she wiggled her fingers next to her core, like a lover, "I don't want you to dine on me just yet. I'd rather you eat me here first before you devour me."

The crazed female shifted as she reached down and pulled Meg's arms out and pinned them over her head. The crazed woman put her knife down as she eyed the witch as she reached down and groped her crotch, her face next Meg's, "How's about I eat your sweet lips and work my way up your body? You will love it so much."

"Here's my counter offer!" Meg replied as she jerked her head forward with all her might, headbutting the crazed female. The woman's nose broke with an audible crack, blood gushed down her face. Meg managed to buck the stunned female off of her body as she reached over for the knife.

A furious growl escaped from Meg as she stabbed her assailant in the neck multiple times. As the female fell over, she eyed the witch coldly as blood gushed from her wounds and stated, "You won't survive the Reset. None shall..."

The crazed female took her last breath but kept her gaze on Meg, which caused her to shutter. She sat up and wiped the blade clean on the dead woman's clothes. A thought occurred to the witch as she stood up:

She knew about the Reset. How is that possible?

Meg wasn't sure that she wanted to know. She tugged her mattress out of the way and opened the door fully. The lifeless corpses haphazardly flopped in the doorway. Meg stepped over them as quietly as she could and padded down the hallway. Her home was ransacked, it had the appearance of a burglary.

This added to the violation that the witch was mentally experiencing. She walked into the kitchen and grabbed a medium size backpack and filled it with food, water bottles, and a cast iron skillet. She rummaged through several drawers, packing knives, can openers, and a few utensils.

The ghost hovered next to the witch and asked, *"Where will you go...?"*

"Any place but here. I need to find a place that I can isolate myself from all of this until it blows over."

"You better take more than this with you...The Reset isn't going to be over for a while..."

Meg glanced at the spectre and asked, "You know that for a fact?" As it nodded, she followed up by asking, "How did the woman know of the Reset?"

"It's in the minds of everyone...Few understand it, while others can't perceive it... The message is different for everyone..."

Meg walked tentatively back into the living room, trying not to let the people outside see her. She crept over to a small closet and gently opened the door. She reached in and dragged out several duffle bags and filled one with extra clothes. She kept glancing at the broken window, feeling exposed in her own home.

She grabbed a small red first aid kit and crept back down the hallway to the bathroom. The witch closed and locked the door as she pulled her shirt off. She stood in front of the mirror and cringed as she examined her wound. It was a good three inches long with blood oozing down her hip.

Meg gasped as she wiped it down with rubbing alcohol poured straight onto it. She vigorously fanned her hand over it to ease the burning and dry it quicker. She grabbed a wash rag and wiped off the blood as the ghost hovered next to the tub.

"Why didn't I hear the message?" Meg asked as she prepped several pieces of gauze with tape, "I never heard one in my head."

"I was the message...I warned you about the Reset..."

Meg glared at the ghost as she placed the bandage on her side, "Gee, you were so informative. How was I to know what to expect when all I got was the same vague message from you?"

"I had no choice in that..." the ghost bristled defensively, *"I did try to convey it as an ominous warning, but you didn't care to hear..."*

"Oh, I heard it. It's all you would say. How can I prepare for an event that I have no information about? Do you realize just how maddening it can be?"

"Talking with you, yes...More than you know...I couldn't say anything and yet all I got was snark in return...ungrateful witch..."

Meg stuck her tongue out at him as she walked back into her room. Despite the dead bodies around her, the witch kept glancing at them, half expecting them to spring back to life as she grabbed a better attire to wear.

Meg tugged her bloody clothes off and let them lie where they fell, much like her attackers. She slipped on a tight form fitting black pants and matching top. Meg leaned against the wall as she tugged on her calf high leather boots. She snatched a black leather jacket and the ghost commented, "*Black again...I was in suspense at what color scheme you would choose next...*"

"Piss off, ghost boy! Black is my favorite color. It matches my heart and soul. Why are you still here anyway?"

"*I've been around for a long time...I don't feel the need to move on...*"

"No, that's not what I'm asking. Why are you still here, with me?"

"*No choice...I was assigned to be with you...*"

"I'm guessing that the one that prevented you from talking is responsible?"

The ghost thought for a moment as Meg walked towards the living room then replied, *"No...Her power isn't that great...The Protector, I mean...I have no idea who squelched me...Trust me, I'd rather move into the light than be around your brooding ass..."*

"I'm starting to wish that you were squelched once more." The witch whispered as she hunkered down upon entering the living room. She watched the shadows pass the broken window, waiting for her opportunity to make her escape.

"I can be your lookout if there's anything else you wish to pack..."

"I need to stuff this," Meg whispered, hoisted up the empty duffle bag, "with food and other things. Let me know if you spot anyone trying to get in here."

"I'll do my best...no guarantees that I can stop them...but I can distract them..."

"How so," the witch inquired as she crawled over to the grocery bags with her duffle bag.

"*They can see and hear me...I might sway them into thinking that I'm haunting this spot...*"

"If that's so, then why didn't you go all spooky on the ones that broke in?" Meg hissed in a hushed tone.

"*They saw Joe and knew that a living person was in here...They wanted to see if there was more residing here...They ignored all my attempts to shoo them off your scent...*"

Meg froze. She looked at the ghost as her mouth gaped open, "My scent? Is that a figure of speech or..."?

The ghost sympathetically gazed at the witch, "*It means the latter that you chose not to say...They can sniff out 'their food' as one of the men stated... It's like they've gone feral in a short period of time...I had to warn you because that's all I could do...*"

The witch continued filling the duffle bag, concern etched over her countenance about this new piece of information. How she could cover her scent, she had no clue. Meg felt overwhelmed as the option of shutting down and not doing anything crept into her mind.

How can I survive if I'm so outmatched and have little to no defenses?

A feminine voice bellowed within her mind, one that had power and authority rumbling through each word, "*Fight or die, witch. It's your choice after all. No one can save you, except yourself.*"

Meg grabbed the sides of her head, cringing painfully as replied, "Who are you and could you tone the power back. I'm getting a migraine."

"*I will try, but you need to choose.*"

"Why? Am I supposed to do something? Why does it matter?"

"*Because I'll not waste my time with a coward.*" The voice bristled, "*You're not the only one out there that needs to survive this.*"

"I think I'm better off on my own." Meg replied as she thought about Joe, "At least I won't get anyone else killed."

"You can't control what others choose to do. You survived and he didn't because you knew what was going on. You were brave enough to fight off five of the Ferals but you can't expect to do this all by yourself. You will fall if you choose the solidarity path."

"Are..." the witch gulped, "are you the Protector that the ghost told me about?"

"I am the one that is needed to save those from humanities machinations. If not for me, more would've died."

"But, why me? What makes me worth saving?"

"You happen to be under my watch because of your innate gifts, as with others like you. Your kind have been charged with enduring the Reset and rebuilding humanity."

"No pressure then," Meg grumbled as she zipped up the duffle bag. She gathered all her bags and waited by the front door. She looked at the ghost and stated, "Let me know when you think it's safe to make a break for the car."

"This I can do, Meg..."

The witch took several deep breaths to calm her anxiety down, not wanting to leave. Unfortunately, she knew that remaining here was no longer an option. The female voice echoed in her mind once more, "*A word of caution. The Ferals aren't the only obstacles you will have to fear.*"

"People like myself that aren't decent. Figures."

"*Yes, and other entities will be more prevalent. So, rely on your intuition because it's there for a reason.*"

"Great. That's all we need now, supernatural threats."

Chapter Seven

The ghost moved silently out of the house, leaving the witch all alone. Meg didn't like the thought of being by herself right now. She felt like she was naked and exposed on a grand stage in front of a packed audience. It's a strange sensation, Meg wasn't used to this kind of vulnerability.

The witch was more of a recluse and independent in every sense of the word, and yet now, she found that she wanted someone, even the ghost, near her. As if it heard her mental musing, the ghost entered the house and stated, *"If you're going to leave...Go now, witch..."*

Meg curtly nodded as she yanked the front door open, her car keys and bat in one hand and her provisions loading down her other arm. The witch didn't use the fob to unlock her SUV, not daring to alert any nearby Ferals of her presence.

She slipped the key into the lock and turned it counter-lock, holding it there so all the locks would unlatch. Meg opened the backseat door and tossed everything in the seat, not caring where the supplies landed. She quietly closed the door and leaned against it, her eyes darting around for movement. Near the sidewalk, she saw the bloody, torn remains of Joe's lifeless body. Several ravens stood on top of him, picking at the loose bits of flesh.

The witch stifled a cry as she yanked the driver's door and slid behind the wheel. She pressed the automatic door lock button, sealing herself in. Meg leaned her forehead against the steering wheel, tears threatened to spill out. A cold hand on her forearm startled her, Meg wild-eyed the ghost and it spoke, *"They're coming...You must go...Now!"*

"Make some noise next time!" The witch yelled as she started the SUV, glaring at the spectre. She shifted into reverse as several Ferals encroached on her vehicle. They were covered in blood and gore, their wild eyes focused on the witch.

The Ferals pounded on the sides of the SUV as Meg bounced a back tire off the curb, jostling her. One jumped on the hood of the SUV and snarled as foamy drool oozed from his mouth, "Step out and let's have some fun. I want to bathe in your entrails while you watch!"

The witch sped down the street as the crazed man punched at the windshield.

"I will show you love like you've never experienced!" The Feral yelled as he licked the dried blood off the windshield, "Pull over and let me in."

"Sure thing," Meg snarked as she turned the corner at a high rate of speed. The Feral growled as he rolled off the hood, rolling several times before ending up in a ditch. Meg didn't dare slow down, let alone look back. She had a feeling that the crazed man was standing up already, looking for his next "*lover*".

"*What's the plan, witch…?*" The ghost asked.

"Find the closest liquor store. Barricade myself inside. Drink myself into oblivion until this all blows over."

"*I'm being serious...*"

"So am I, ghost boy." Meg replied with a deadpan expression.

"That's not much of a plan..."

"It's the only one that sounds great to me. Besides, I figure you would like it there. You know, with all the *spirits* in one place."

"Of all the people in the world...I had to get saddled to a drunken witch..."

Meg glared at the ghost, "So, tell me, ghost boy. When you die, do you lose your sense of humor along with your physical body?"

The spectre bristled, *"You will discover that for yourself, one day...I have a name, you know..."*

The witch snorted, "I'm sure you do. Though you never said it, just your repeating message. So, what do I call you?"

"Eric..."

"Eric?" Meg stated, "Huh, I figured it would be something like Reginald or Francis, not so mundane."

"Just as mundane as yours, I'm afraid..." The ghost smirked.

Meg's mouth gaped open as she glanced at Eric, who was now chuckling, "Ha ha. Very funny, Eric. At least I know you have a rudimentary form of humor in your wispy body."

"Where are you going…?"

"Like I have a plan," the witch honestly answered, "I'm making it up on the fly. Aren't you supposed to help me stay alive? Aren't you supposed to guide me to a safe place? Like - oh fuck!"

Meg slammed on the brakes, causing the SUV to skid to a halt. The street was swarming with Ferals, mutilated bodies were strung out all around. Ferals were on rooftops, desecrating their victims in both creative and unimaginable ways. It reminded Meg of a zombie movie. Many sickening eyes fixated on the witch as Eric stated, *"I recommend not going this way...It doesn't bode well for you, witch..."*

"You think?" Meg retorted as the Ferals were jumping off the roofs of houses, rushing towards them. She put her vehicle in reverse but noticed that they were surrounded by the crazed horde.

"Do something or this will be your final resting place, Meg..."

The SUV shook and rocked as the first wave of Ferals reached them. Meg repeatedly pressed the automatic lock button, hoping that none would make it inside.

"Drive or die…"

The witch pressed down on the gas pedal, backing over some of her attackers. The vehicle lurched and bounced like it was on an icy, pothole road. Meg couldn't see out the back window, bodies obscured the view as more Ferals climbed on the SUV.

"Look out, Meg…!" Eric shouted as he saw several Ferals run at her door, carrying another person like a battering ram. The person's head bashed into the window, shattering most of it and surprising the witch. She screamed as hands punched through, sending shards of glass everywhere, and grabbed her by her hair and shirt.

As Meg struggled to free herself from her assailants, one of the Ferals reached in and pressed the automatic door lock. The door was flung open and several hands reached in, dragging the witch out of her vehicle.

Meg cried out in pain as her body was violently tossed to the pavement as hands groped her. She could hear the sound of fabric tearing and felt the tips of shoes slamming into her body. She moaned in agony as fingers snaked into her hair, pulling her up to a standing position.

Several fists struck Meg in her face and abdomen as the crazed people cheered. The witch hoped that these monsters would end her life quickly, but from what she witnessed today, she knew that the rest of her short life would be filled with pain and suffering.

Meg was forcefully pinned to the back end of a nearby truck as the last remnants of her clothes were discarded, save her boots. The metal of the truck scorched the witch's bare skin as a female straddled her writhing form. The ghost hovered next to her as the Feral woman leaned down and roughly pressed her lips against Meg's as she banged the back of her head against the truck bed.

"Help is coming..." Eric stated with a sympathetic visage, *"Just fight them, Meg..."*

"No one is going to save her, dead thing," the woman snarled as she groped the dazed witch's core. "You can stay there and watch us play with your girlfriend."

Meg screamed as she felt teeth piercing into her thighs while several rough fingers violated both her core and ass. She gasped as she felt something sharp repeatedly cut her stomach. The Feral woman pulled Meg's head up by her hair and got eye to eye with her, her breath smelled of rotting meat and eggs.

She forced Meg's eyelids open as she cooed, "You're so pretty. Prettier than me. That's why I'm going to make your experience last as long as I can. I think I will peel this pretty face off and parade myself with it on. How does that sound?"

"Just...kill me..." Meg rasped as she moaned in pain, unable to focus on the mad woman, "have fun...with me...after I'm...gone..."

The Feral woman turned and snarled at the other Ferals like a predator protecting its kill, causing the others to shy back. She glared wildly until she and the witch were alone and then she banged Meg's head against the truck bed several more times before replying, "That's not how this works. You don't suffer like I do, so I have to make you feel *everything*. You think that you're better than me? I hate everything that you are, which is why you must suffer. Doesn't that sound like fun?"

Meg's head lulled to the side as her attacker proceeded to lick her face as she roughly inserted her fingers into her core. The witch's swollen eyes blearily focused on the ghost as she heard him say, "*They are here...*"

Several blood curdling howls filled the air, causing the Feral woman to pause. The sounds of running footfall echoed everywhere around the two as Ferals sprinted by. With strength that defied her small stature, the crazed female picked up Meg and carried her limp body out of the truck. She ran down the road with her plaything, causing Meg's head to jerk and bob uncontrollably.

The witch hears a familiar voice in her, calmly telling her, *"Fear not, the howling. They're your only hope of survival, witch."*

The Feral woman abruptly stopped as she snapped, "This one is mine! You can't have her!"

Meg heard snarls all around her as her captor growled back in response. The witch felt the Feral woman lurch backwards and then a pair of warm arms ripped her out of the woman's grasp.

Meg vaguely wondered who had her now. Whomever it was didn't attempt to molest her, yet. She smelled an aroma of cedar, sage, and blood. Meg didn't open her eyes, but managed to mutter, "End me now...I beg you..."

A feminine voice cooed, "Shh, I've got you. That *woman* won't hurt you ever again."

"Don't care...kill me..." Meg whimpered as tears streamed down her face.

"Rest, Meg...You're not with the Ferals now...Your time to die isn't now..." Eric replied and then he spoke to her savior, *"Take her car there...It has supplies within it...It will make it easier to get her to safety..."*

"Barbara!" The female barked out over the snarls and screams as she opened the side door of the SUV, "I need a driver!"

Meg barely made out their conversation.

"I'm on it, Mia."

"Are there any other survivors here?"

"Other than this one?" Barbara sadly replied, "No. Most are dying or dead. The pack is giving mercy to those that need it."

"Damn," Mia spat as she sat Meg's body down in the backseat. She shifted some of the witch's bags around so that she could sit in the back with her. The strange woman closed the door as Barbara used a tattered shirt to clean most of the shattered glass off the driver's seat.

Mia cuddled Meg against her as she examined her wounds. She caught the scent of cinnamon amongst the metallic aroma of

117

blood. Barbara slipped in behind the wheel, closed the door, and shifted the SUV into gear. She looked in the rearview mirror and asked, "Can you tell if she is one of us or a Blissful Victim?"

"I can't say for sure," Mia stroked Meg's blood-soaked black hair gently as she noticed the ghost appear next to her, "but I suspect that she's one of us. What say you, ghost? Is she your charge?"

Meg heard Eric state just as she blacked out, "*I wouldn't be with the witch if she wasn't...*"

Chapter Eight

The witch thrashed around for a few minutes before crying out in terror as she sat up. A cold sweat covered her entire body. She felt sore and her entire body ached all over. Meg looked down and saw that she was lying on a twin size mattress, covered with a soft fleece blanket.

She was in a large, dimly lit room that had beds lining each of the concrete walls, all were occupied. Meg kicked the blanket off and immediately regretted it as pain coursed through her body. She squeezed her eyes tightly shut, letting the wave of pain subsided.

Meg saw that she was dressed in an oversized shirt that went halfway down her bandaged thighs. She had an IV line in her wrist that had several bags hanging from the metal stand. Her boots sat next to the side of her bed, next to a small wooden crate that had several bottles of water sitting on top of it. The witch tugged her shirt up and examined her body. It was covered in bruises and where there weren't bruises, bandages stood out. A stark reminder of the trauma that she endured.

A metal door to her right opened and a young woman entered with a tray in hand. Moans and murmurs filled the room as she walked around, checking each person by placing a hand on their foreheads and checking pulses.

Am I in a hospital?

The woman turned and looked at Meg. She seemed surprised and caught off guard, but she smiled warmly at the witch. Meg reached over and grabbed a water bottle and opened it. She slowly sipped the warm water, the liquid soothed her dry, scratchy throat.

The woman came over and sat down on the edge of the bed, compassionately smiling at Meg. She put her hand on the witch's forehead and asked, "How are you feeling this evening?"

"Like a turd dropped in a food processor," Meg stated as she hugged herself, wincing, "Where am I?"

"It's Meg, right?" When the witch nodded, the woman continued, "You're safe in our facility. You were brought here about a week ago. Your wounds were extensive and you had a high fever, along with an infection."

"Oh good," Meg replied sarcastically, "and here I thought this was my Airbnb stay down in the Cancun. Who the hell are you?"

"I'm Dr. Arnica and I'm one of the reasons that you're still alive," she stated as she stood up, checking Meg's IV bags, "I don't have all the medical supplies that I'm used to having on hand, but I'm sure that you will be fine to move around after this bag is finished."

"Cool, so I can leave here once it's done?"

The doctor paused as she eyed the witch, "I don't see why not, but I need to ask. What do you recall happening to you before you woke up here?"

Meg thought long and hard, her brow furrowed, as the sound of the metal door opened again, "I'm not sure what's real anymore, doc."

"Tell me, Meg."

"Death. Everywhere I look, I see people dying."

"What else?"

"People acting strange. They're either looking for ways to die and those on the opposite end of the spectrum, wanting to maim and kill. It can't be real, can it?"

"Unfortunately, it is, Meg," Mia answered as she neared the bed, carrying a folding chair. She straddled it once she set it next to the bed. The scent of cedar and sage wafted in the air, causing Meg to eye the woman and feeling like she knew her.

"Do I know you?" Meg asked, then added, "Your perfume? I swear that I've smelled it before coming here."

"No, but subconsciously I think you do remember who I am. My name is Mia. I was one of the ones responsible for bringing you here."

"I see," the witch replied, still trying to remember the woman before her, "Your name sounds vaguely familiar and yet, I don't recall you bringing me to this place."

"You went through a great deal of stress and physical trauma," Dr Arnica chirped up,

"The shock of everything that transpired left you in a kind of fugue state. With time, the memories will surface but for now, your brain is suppressing them, like a defense mechanism. Those that this doesn't happen to, end up going mad because they can't handle their new reality. It's a trend that I've been seeing lately."

"And what new reality is that?"

Mia stood up as she said, "I can fill her in on this if you're done here, doctor."

Dr Arnica sighed before walking over to the next bed, "Keep an eye on her and be prepared if she has total recall."

"Noted." Mia answered as she sat down on the side of the bed. She brushed several strands of hair from Meg's face, "At least you're not as pale as the ghost that hangs out with you when we first met."

"My ghost?" The witch looked around and then saw him coalesce at the end of her bed. Meg snorted, "You mean my broken record?"

Eric looked at the witch as a smile crossed his face, *"I see that she's finally awake..."*

"Whoa, when did *you* develop a vocabulary, ghost boy? About fucking time!"

Mia observed the ghost as it moved over to the side of the bed. He wrapped his arms across his ethereal chest as he huffed, *"Since I can recall...I see that you still possess a disposition that's as warm and cuddly as a frozen cactus plant..."*

Meg rolled her eyes, "Piss off! I only recall you droning on about being prepared for the Reset for weeks on end."

"She doesn't remember yet," Mia spoke as she saw the quizzical look on Eric's face, "but I have a feeling that she will soon."

"Hello?" Meg waved her hand, causing the IV tubing to whip around, "I'm right here. I can hear you talking about me, you know?"

Mia scooted up the bed, getting closer to the witch. Meg wearily asked as she closely watched the stranger, "What are you doing?"

"Am I making you uncomfortable?" Mia asked. Meg nodded her head quickly as her heart raced. Her breathing came in short spurts and anxiety flooded her mind.

"Good because I'm going to ask that you bear with me. I think that I can help you remember because you recall my 'perfume', as you put it."

"Please don't come any closer," Meg pleaded. The witch didn't understand what was causing her to feel so anxious about the woman. Mia was a physically fit woman with long blonde hair and visage like a porcelain doll, but her closeness seemed to set off alarm bells in Meg's brain.

"Don't hate me for doing this to you, Meg, but I need to know if you are going to be useful or simply fall apart when you remember."

"What do you - Hey! Hands off me, bitch!"

Mia held the witch in her arms, keeping her in place. She pulled out a small vial from her pocket that contained a dark liquid inside.

Eric inspected it and his charge as he asked, "*Is this a wise course of action...? She may not recover if you do this...Is it truly worth the risk...?*"

"I don't like it any more than you or her, but it has to be this way. The Reset isn't slowing down and we need all able bodies for the coming fight."

"If you think I'm drinking whatever that stuff is, then be ready for a fight, blondie!"

"I'm more than prepared, but I'm not going to force it down your throat," Mia replied as she popped the lid off the vial, "I need you to smell it. That's all."

Meg squirmed, "Why restrain me, if that's all?"

"Because you *will* react to it," Mia stated with a hint of regret, "This will cause that little gap in your memory to hopefully flood open. I want to keep you from hurting yourself."

"Shouldn't the doctor be here for this?" The witch asked, her eyes widened as the vial came closer to her face.

"She's still in here and will be coming back by because I'm more than likely going to need her help. Now, sniff and remember."

The witch feared the contents for reasons that she couldn't explain and yet, she didn't inhale it. Mia growled impatiently, "Sniff it or I'll be forced to trace this liquid on your upper lip! Hmm, maybe I'll do just that."

"Please don't," Meg pleaded, unsure why it bothered her, "I'll comply. It's just that...I'm afraid and I don't know why. I'm not sure I want to remember."

"Actually," Dr Arnica stated as she sat down on the other side of the bed, "unconsciously, you know why. There's a good reason that this is an effective method. The downside of it is that you will recall all those nasty events that occurred to you during the Reset. If you can recover from it, that remains to be seen."

"That's not very reassuring, doc."

"It's all we have," Mia interjected, "I'd rather have you breakdown in here than outside of these walls, where you would be vulnerable. I understand your hesitancy, but we don't have time for it. Either recall and endure, like the rest of us or go mad, in which case we will be forced to give you mercy."

"No pressure," Meg snarked as she took several deep breaths, and nodded, "Do it then, before I chicken out."

Mia slowly moved the vial back and forth under Meg's nostrils, letting the rank aroma assail her senses. She could feel the witch tensing up, her face scrunched up like she was going to be sick.

"Get ready, doc," Mia commanded.

Meg hated the aroma from the contents of the vial. It was a horrible smell, consisting of rotting meat and eggs. She knew that odor and with it, came all the memories that her brain had locked away. The witch screamed hysterically, thrashing around as her eyes wildly darted everywhere.

"Go play in the street if you want that sort of action! What the hell is going on! Why Trevor? Joe! Fuck! Here's my counter offer!" Meg cried out, reliving those terrible moments once again, "Oh Gods they're everywhere! I'm surrounded! No, no, no! Just...kill me...have fun... with me...after I'm... gone..."

The witch wailed loudly as the tears flowed unabated down her face. Her entire body shook and spasmed, as though she were having a seizure. Both Mia and the doctor held her down, but did allow her some bodily movements as the worst of the fits lessened.

"End me now...I beg you..."

Mia softly spoke as she replied, "Shh, I've got you. That *woman* won't hurt you ever again."

"Don't care...kill me..." Meg whimpered as she looked between the two women holding her. Mia motioned at the doctor and they adjusted the witch's position on the bed so that it could barely accommodate two people lying on it. Meg's hands were clenched into fists as she held onto the fitted sheet for dear life, making it difficult to move her.

Mia maneuvered herself down on the bed, lying next to the quivering witch. She calmly spoke to Meg, knowing that there was a chance that she wasn't going to hear her, let alone comprehend, "Meg, I know that you're in the shit right now. I'm not sure if you'll understand what I'm going to do. I'm going to lay here and hold you against me. I'm hoping that since you remember my 'perfume', it may help you know that you're safe in my arms."

Meg babbled incoherently, her body shaking like a blade of grass in a windstorm. Mia pulled the witch in a full body embrace, stroking her silky black hair and damp back.

"Just relax and breathe in my scent. You're in safe arms. I'm not going anywhere, Meg. I'm right here."

"You got this one?" Dr Arnica asked.

Mia curtly nodded. The doctor let go of Meg and stood up. She remained standing there, just in case the witch had another violent fit before leaving. She called over her shoulder, "Page me on the intercom if you need anything else. I won't be far. I can send a few more people in, if you'd like."

"I think we are good," Mia replied, "But just to be safe, have someone standing outside. I'd rather not traumatize this one further."

As the doctor left the room, Mia kept a firm but soothing hold on Meg, their bodies planted against one another like lovers. Meg could smell the woman's scent, which was way more pleasing than the stuff in the vial.

Sage and cedar.

Her panic ebbed slightly as she focused on Mia and weakly asked, "Were you the one that saved from...umm, that woman?"

"Yes, I was present," the woman stated, "There were others too, so I can't take all the credit."

"But…" Meg paused as she inhaled deeply, "they weren't the ones carrying my pathetic ass to safety. So, for that, thank you."

"You're welcome," Mia beamed a bright smile, "This is why I'm the one doing this. Keeping you company, that is. If you're feeling better, I can explain it to you."

Meg rested her head against Mia's chest, inhaling her scent. She thought about it as she chewed on her bottom lip nervously. She pulled herself closer to Mia, not wanting to let her go.

Am I ready for this? I doubt it.

"I'm not sure if I'm ready, but I'd rather you just rip the band-aid off and let me have it."

"Very well," Mia said as she retrieved the glass vial, "Can you guess what's in here?" The witch shook her, wearily eyeing it, "This is what we call Feral goo. It's that brown foamy substance that comes from their mouth. We use it as a trigger object for people, like you, that block out the unspeakable horrors you experienced. Others tend to be so traumatized that they refuse to acknowledge us, let alone speak. Its pungent odor is one that many can't forget, which is why it's so effective."

Meg gazed at the brown liquid, shuttering, "How did you get it?"

"The hard way," Mia answered as she slipped it back into her pocket, "The Feral has to be alive so you can imagine the difficulty required to harvest it. It dries up and breaks down, even stored samples like the one I have. Now that the unpleasant part has been," Mia shook her hand repeatedly, "err, cliff notes explained, I shall tell you why I'm in bed cuddling with you."

"I think I understand that part," Meg replied, "My brain is interpreting that I'm safe because it recalls your scent. Matching it with the one who rescued and got me to safety."

"Pretty much the gist of it. I don't fully understand all of this, but it does work."

"Tell me about yourself and this place. Where am I exactly?"

"Not much to say, except that I'm like you and yet, we're different. You're a witch and I'm a shifter."

Chapter Nine

Meg's crystal blue eyes narrowed at the woman, "Seriously, a shifter?"

"As serious as the Ferals that attacked you," Mia replied.

"Yeah," the witch snorted, "and I'm the queen of Sauvie Island! Shifters aren't a real thing. They're just mythical creatures used as fodder for cheap movies and crumby romance novels."

"You doubt me and yet you claim to be a witch?"

"Of course! What does me being a witch have to do with it?"

"We're both supernatural beings. You should know about my kind, as well as other entities."

Meg snarked, "You're so right! I'm a witch, which means I should know everything about everything! I didn't go to Hogwarts so I didn't receive a proper education in witchcraft nor did a wand choose me."

Mia eyed the witch for a moment. She cocked her head and asked, "Are you serious? Haven't you ever cast spells? Surely, you have some spells at your disposal that you can fight with, don't you?"

Meg pushed away from the shifter and sat up, her back against the wall, "No. Just karma spells and other circle rituals. The stuff that you're talking about sounds like the crap you see in the movies. Magic can't be seen."

Mia chuckled as she rolled out of the bed. She walked around the bed and stood next to the ghost. She crossed her arms across her chest as her facial features changed. Her eyes glowed as her irises turned yellow and predatory as she peeled off her clothes. Mia opened her mouth, revealing sharp canines. Meg watched on in utter fascination as the woman shifted into a wolf with brown and black fur, right before her eyes.

"Oh, my Gods, you're beautiful!"

Mia padded over and nuzzled the witch and licked her face, causing Meg to squeal. She caressed the wolf's pelt, noting how soft it felt. Meg locked her gaze with Mia as she sighed, "I wish I could do this. I think it's amazing and cool. Unfortunately, I'm just a cantankerous witch with no magic to show you."

The wolf growled as she backed away from the witch, slowly shifting back into her human form. Mia stood fully erect with her hands on her hips, shaking her head, "You still don't get it? I showed this transformation to prove that you *do* have magic at your disposal that can be seen by all now."

Meg barely paid attention as she eyed Mia's skyclad form, "I'm not going to lie. You're beautiful this way too, Mia."

The witch's eyes widened as the words from the shifter registered in her awe fogged mind, just as she heard the ghost snicker, *"She catches on quick, doesn't she?"*

Meg looked down at her hands and asked, "Are...are you saying that I can transform...like you do?"

"Okay...Maybe not that quick, apparently..."

Meg glared as she stuck her tongue out at the ghost while Mia chuckled as she got dressed. She sat down on the side of the bed as she grabbed the witch's hand tenderly, "I know that you can't because you're not a shifter like me. We can smell shifters, even in human form. Alas, sweet Meg, you're not one of us. Besides, your scent is unique and speaks of your witchery heritage."

"Really?" Meg sniffed her clothes, "What is my scent? I don't smell anything."

Eric sniffed as he flew up from the witch's feet and slowly made his way up to her face with a smirk, "*Cheap wine, sarcasm, and bitchy resentment is what I smell...*"

"Ha ha, very funny, ghost boy," the witch grumbled. She wanted to wrap her arms across her chest and sulk, but the shifter refused to relinquish her hand. Mia lifted Meg's hand up to her nose, never taking her gaze off the witch, causing her to blush slightly. The shifter inhaled with her eyes closed and smiled.

Meg held her breath as she unconsciously nibbled on her bottom lip, waiting for the shifter's response. Mia opened her eyes as she softly pressed her lips against the back of the witch's hand, seductively smirked,

"Cinnamon. I can never get enough of that scent."

"My assessment is more accurate, Mia..." Eric commented as he hovered ethereally at the end of the bed.

"Hush! Don't ruin the moment!" Meg hissed as the ghost laughed. He pointed at the witch, *"I rest my case..."*

Mia let go of Meg's hand and stood up. She looked at the IV bags and commented, "Once the doctor takes you off the fluids, I'll come get you and give you a proper tour of our facility."

The shifter leaned down and pressed her lips against Meg's forehead. They both inhaled each other's scents as Mia said, "Get some more rest, witch. You're going to need it for what I have in store for you."

"I wish you would stay here with me," Meg replied, feeling foolish so she meekly added, "I know, that sounds sappy and weak. I don't know why I feel like this."

The shifter hesitated leaning back, her eyes drawn to the witch's melancholy gaze.

She caressed her fingers along Meg's jawline, "I understand, but I have other matters to attend to. Don't worry, witch, I'm not going to be gone long."

"Please, call me Meg, *shifter*." The witch said playfully.

"I will, Meg," the shifter answered as she walked towards the door. She looked over her shoulder as she grabbed the door handle and added with a wink, "if you will refer to me as Mia."

Meg slid down into her bed as the door closed. She covered her body with her blanket. It still had Mia's scent on it, much to her delight. The witch rolled on her side, watching the door. She stuck a tuff of the fabric under her nose as Eric appeared next to her.

"Don't worry, Meg…She will be back shortly..."

"Are you sure?" The ghost nodded so she added, "What makes you so certain? I'm just an uneducated witch with zero skills or talents. Why would she even bother?"

Eric replied with a smirk, "*Because she said she would be...Mia has been watching over you ever since her group saved your grumpy ass...*"

Meg watched the spectre, expecting him to laugh at her some more, but he didn't. She never was this self-conscious about herself. The witch knew that her body was covered in scars from her encounters with the Ferals. Mia had seen her at her most vulnerable, maimed and humiliated beyond imagination, and yet, the shifter wanted to be around her.

She nodded slowly as she closed her eyes. Eric moved away and stated, "*Rest well, witch...I'll watch over you until your hero returns...*"

"Piss off, ghost boy," Meg murmured, smiling softly as sleep took a hold over her.

Meg stirred as she felt someone touching her arm. She jerked awake, uncertain where she was at. "Please, don't hurt me!" The witch blurted out, wild eyed.

"Ahhh," the man jumped, throwing his hands up submissively, "Sorry. I'm not going to hurt you. I'm trying to unhook your IV so you move about freely."

"Oh," Meg replied sheepishly as he slowly moved his hands down.

"May I remove your IV line, Meg?"

"Sure," the witch gulped as she placed her arm in his callous hands, "Sorry that I freaked out. I'm not normally like this."

"Understandable, given what you went through at the hands of the Ferals. I should've tried harder to wake you up but you wouldn't rouse. I'm Jace, by the way."

"I told you that she was a difficult witch..." Eric commented as he watched the attendant swiftly remove the needle from his charge's wrist.

"Hi Jace," Meg said as she ignored the ghost and searched the room. She bit her bottom lip in disappointment, "Have you seen Mia?"

Jace wrapped a bandage over a small cotton ball, "She's been in and out of the facility today. Her pack goes out to scout and recruit others like us." He sighed heavily, "No one came back with them today."

Meg's lips parted, realizing just how lucky she was when she was found by Mia's pack. She wanted to make it up to the shifter, but didn't exactly know how. Jace's scent wafted to nostrils as he removed the empty IV bags from the stand.

Spearmint.

"Are you a shifter or something like that?"

"Who me?" Jace asked.

"No...She was talking to me... Obviously..." Eric smirk as he hovered ethereally by his side.

Jace grinned as the witch attempted to swat at the ghost, "No, I'm not that lucky. I'm a healer. I have been my whole life, which is why I became a nurse. Now, how about you try getting up and do some walking around."

The witch nodded in agreement. She pushed the blanket off and gingerly sat on the side of the bed. Her body ached all over, the bandages tugged on her skin as she stood up.

She winced as she took her first few steps. Jace walked next to the witch, he motioned to the metal door, "If you need a shower or just need to go to the bathroom, it's just outside the door there."

They walked around the room several times, Meg couldn't help but look at the other patients. Each one seemed in worse shape than the last one. Her nurse noticed and said, "I'm not sure if anyone else will survive like you. Only time will tell..."

Meg's eyes teared up as her body complained for a respite. She trudged forward as her bed came into view. The metal door burst open, a burly man stormed in, carrying a blood caked teenage boy. His clothes were in shambles and his prone body hung limp in the man's massive arms. The kid reminded the witch of the young stock boy that kept referring to her as 'his angel'.

"Jace!" The man barked out, "I need a bed, fast!"

The nurse looked all over the room; each bed was occupied.

"Give him mine," Meg pointed as she collapsed to her knees, "I'm well enough that I won't need it."

The man curtly nodded as he rushed over and gently placed the kid on the bed. Dr Arnica, along with several other people rushed in to examine the new patient. Meg hung her head, panting and not wanting to look at the teenager as many voices filled the room.

The witch felt arms drape around her shoulders and her senses were assailed by a familiar but pleasant odor.

Cedar and sage.

"Come with me, Meg. We will only get in their way," Mia said as she lifted the witch up to her feet. The burly man paced nervously back and forth by the door; his eyes glowed as he watched the doctor's team work on the kid. Mia called out, "Come along, Axel, there's no more you can do for him."

"No!" Axel growled as he showed signs of transformation. Meg saw razor sharp claws extending from the tips of his fingers, his face distorting, taking on more ape-like features. "You got to be around *your* witch when she came and she survived! Why can't I do the same for the psychic? I can't take it! I can't lose another one, Mia!"

"I get what you're saying," Mia said, trying to sooth him, "I'm growing weary of all this needless death. But I think-"

"If this one dies," Axel snarled as he pointed one his deadly claws at the witch, "*she's* next! Along with everyone in this room!"

Doctor Arnica and her team paused as they turned to look at Axel, their eyes wide and full of fear. Mia put her body in front of the witch, baring her teeth as she retorted, "Mind your emotions and that tongue of yours. Get out of here now! Go for a run in the training room or blow off some steam."

"Why should I?" He towered over Mia menacing.

The shifter held her ground as she looked up into his angry eyes, "If you don't, the boy *will* die. Your attitude is scaring the ones that can save him. Every second that they don't care for him means certain death. Do you want to be responsible for it?"

Meg watched on. She could see the emotional turmoil raging in Axel. The witch felt bad for him, but at the same time, she silently prayed that the teenager would survive. For some reason, she was the target to spew his anger and frustration on. Axel roared and then dropped down to his knees, eyeing the medical staff. They attempted to assess the boy's wounds, but kept glancing at him in fear.

The burly man slumped his shoulders, sobbing, "I just don't want to lose another one, Mia."

She placed her hands on his broad shoulders. Mia rested her forehead against his and softly said, "I know, which is why you've got to leave and let them do what they do best."

Axel nodded as Mia stepped back. He stood up and went to leave but paused as Mia threatened, "Good choice, but if you dare attempt any harm against Meg, I will tear your throat out. Got it?"

He turned around and glared at her and the witch, making Meg want to flee.

"No promises. He dies, her life is forfeit," Axel grumbled as he stormed out of the room. The shifter turned her attention to the medical team and said as she pulled Meg towards the door, "We'll leave you to it. I'll have guards placed outside so Axel won't trouble you."

"See to it," Dr Arnica angrily replied, "I can't save everyone if my people are being threatened. Keep that *man* on a tight leash."

"Understood, doctor," the shifter replied as she closed the metal door. She let out a sigh as she shook her head, "Sorry about Axel. He's not handling the Reset well and, if you hadn't noticed, he's quite the hothead."

"What did I do to deserve his stink eye?"

Mia walked over to a phone on the wall and lifted the receiver off the hook. She looked at the witch sympathetically, "You're one of the few people that has survived thus far. He's taking all the losses too personally. He views you as a stark reminder of all the failures to save others on his part."

147

Meg shrugged her shoulders as she leaned against the cold concrete wall for support, "Maybe you should've let the Ferals keep me. If I'm the reason for the strife, maybe I should leave and take my chances."

"Don't you say that, ever again," Mia pressed a red button, "Just because Axel is being an ass doesn't mean you or anyone needs to die. He needs to get it out of his system."

A voice on the receiver answered, "*Jacob here.*"

"Jacob. Mia here."

A shuffling of papers and a gasp was heard, "*Oh, um! Yes, Mia! How can I help?*"

"Axel is acting crazed and has just threatened the lives of everyone in the medical ward. I need guards down here, NOW!"

"*Right away, Mia!*" He stated as he muffled the receiver, barking orders, "*The twins will be there.*"

"Good. Thanks Jacob."

"*No problem. Umm, Mia?*"

"Yes?" The shifter asked, knowing full well the question on his lips before he spoke.

"How's your witch?"

"I'm escorting her to her quarters. She will need someone on guard at her door, at all times."

"Heard and understood. I'll have Barbara begin the watch over your witch."

Chapter Ten

Mia rolled her eyes as she hung up the phone. She smiled brightly as she sauntered over to the witch. Meg let the shifter assist her down the long corridor to a wheelchair. Mia motioned for her to sit, but Meg scoffed, "I'm not an invalid! I can walk under my own power."

"You're having difficulty moving on your own. You should park the pride and let me help you to your room. It's quite a ways away."

"*Stubborn as always...Good luck getting her in that...*" The ghost tsked as he coalesced in front of the women.

Meg stuck her tongue out at the spectre and tried to reason with the shifter, "I see that you want me to use it so how's about a compromise. I push it like a little old man's walker and if I struggle, I will let you push me around."

Mia stroked her chin, mulling it over. "Oh fine. I suppose it will be good for you to walk more." she acquiesced but sternly added, "But if you struggle and try fighting me, so help me I will duct tape your ass to the chair. Got it, Meg?"

Meg grasped the handles of the wheelchair. She grinned as she saluted Mia, "Got it, my bossy wolf."

The shifter scowled at the witch, but as she turned and walked slightly ahead of her, Mia half smiled. They walked in tandem together, the shifter kept a watchful on Meg for signs of fatigue. The facility, Meg learned, was an abandoned military base that became outdated long ago. The supernatural beings had been using it for years, upgrading and remodeling it the best that they could without attracting too much attention.

Mia told her that the exterior remains the same, in the hopes that its rundown appearance would deter the notice from the public eye. Occasionally, a group of teenagers or ghost hunters tried to break in. Guards greeted them, telling them that it was government property and that they could be shot for trespassing.

"How did you manage the ones that saw through the ruse?" Meg asked as they entered a decent size room that had couches, a couple of pool tables, several pinball and arcade games, as well as a huge flat screen TV.

"It was difficult in the beginning," Mia answered honestly, "I won't lie. People died before we were able to truly contribute. It was difficult being here and unable to interact with the physical world."

Confused, the witch paused and looked at the shifter, "Wait, wait, wait. Are you saying that you were like Eric over there? More on a different plane of existence?"

"Exactly, but now with the Reset, I can be seen," the shifter placed her hand on the witch's shoulder, "and physically interact with the people here."

Meg softly smiled as her knees slightly buckled. Mia gasped as she reached out and helped her up.

"I'd say that she's spent and in need of a break from walking..." the ghost smirked,

"Question is: will she fight you about sitting in the dreaded wheelchair...?"

"Piss off, ghost boy!" Meg hissed as she let the shifter maneuver her into the wheelchair, "Thanks. See? I told you that I wouldn't fight her."

"I've silently observed you for weeks, Meg...We both know that you have a stubborn streak as large as the Columbia Gorge..."

"Gee, thanks," the witch groaned as she sat down, gladly inhaling Mia's scent. It helped ebb some of the ire she felt, but the ghost wasn't finished.

"Of course, it doesn't compare to the size of the gaping cavity between her ears... That's one void I choose not to look at...I'm pleasantly surprised she's survived this long..."

"You're an ass, Eric," Meg grumbled as she crossed her arms across her chest as the shifter pushed her forward. "I should create white light and force your spectral ass to move on so I can have a moment of peace."

The ghost floated in front of the women while flying backwards. He let out an ethereal

153

growl that caught the witch by surprise, "*I'd gladly walk into it, but even that won't work on me, at this time...You're stuck with me, whether you like it or not...*"

"You two star-crossed lovers stop it," Mia intervened before the conversation got worse, "He's right. You can't move him on." Before Eric could chime in, the shifter cut him off with a predatory glare, "That being said, he should be a little nicer to you."

"*I'm only conveying what I couldn't for weeks...*" The ghost whined, "*You can't imagine what it's like living with her without the option of free speech...*"

"There's never a good excuse to verbally abuse anyone," Mia countered as she put a possessive hand on Meg's shoulder, "You might be protected from being moved on, but that doesn't mean that you can't be *shredded.*"

Meg looked up at Mia and noticed that her eyes were glowing, her inner wolf itching to come out. The witch glanced at Eric, who looked paler than usual. Worry was etched across his translucent face. She wasn't exactly

154

sure what the shifter meant by 'shredding', but the threat seemed to terrify the ghost.

"You wouldn't dare..."

"Try me and find out. I have no qualms about tearing your spectral form apart!" Mia snarled.

Meg put her hand on top of the shifter's hand. She squeezed it wearily as she said, "It's okay. He's not worth it," She leaned her head against Mia's forearm and lamented with a sigh, "Everything he said is spot on. I'm not worth anything to anyone. Those that meant something to me are more than likely dead or a Feral. There's no need to make a fuss."

Eric's lips parted as the shifter got in her face, her eyes still glowing. She gently cupped Meg's face, "You don't mean that. Everyone means something to someone, whether they know it or not. Don't let his words affect you."

Meg cast her teary eyes down, avoiding the shifter's intense stare, "I want to eat something and go rest in my quarters. Can we possibly do that?"

Mia pressed her lips together as she curtly nodded, "Sure. I could use a nice meal." She released the witch's face and swiftly moved behind her. Mia scowled at Eric as she hastened past him. As they left the rec room, a pair of tall pale figures waited patiently for them to pass by.

"Mia," the duo greeted her at the same time.

"Victor. Gloria."

"Axel being Axel again?" Gloria impassively asked as her gaze fell on Meg, her southern drawl pronounced.

"Unfortunately. Do what you must. He's not allowed to enter the medical bay."

"Is this the little witch your pack brought back?" Victor asked, his accent thick, bespeaking of Eastern European lineage. He leaned down and stroked Meg's cheek softly as his gaze raked over, causing the witch to shutter.

"This is Meg and I ask that you treat her with the same respect you give to me and bring no harm to her. Understand?"

156

Victor stood back up, his sky-blue eyes twinkled as he half smiled, "I will endeavor to abide. I'm not going to eat her," his lips curled back, revealing fangs that he slowly ran his tongue over, "unless she wants me to."

Gloria grabbed Victor's arm and tugged him to move as Mia's eyes glowed, "Come along, you. We have a job to do. It was nice to see you up and around, Meg."

"Same here," Meg replied as the pair marched quietly into the rec room, "I think? What exactly were those two?"

The shifter pushed the wheelchair forward, "I figured that it was obvious. They're vampires. If anyone can stop Axel, it's those two."

Meg nodded as she grazed her hand on her cheek where the vampire's fingers had touched, "So, vampires are a real thing? I thought that was Hollywood crap."

"Their kind is extremely rare here. The twins are like the Hollywood trope you've heard about, except that the sun doesn't destroy them. Your world has more energy vampires than bloodsuckers. You're better off resigning yourself to the fact that what you considered as myth or Hollywood make-believe is real."

Meg felt overwhelmed as they turned the corner and entered a cafeteria. It had two dozen long tables with individual chairs. Embedded in the surrounding walls were tables. One section had glass that one could view a small terrace that had several fountains and benches and in the middle was a wooden pergola that had ivy growing on it. The witch smiled, thinking that it would be nice to check out as she got better.

Mia pushed them up to the counter where they were met by an elderly woman. She smiled jovially as she asked, "What will our new recruit have today, Mia?"

Meg stammered, "I-I don't know. What do you have?"

"Depends," the elderly woman coyly replied.

"Depends on what?"

Mia leaned down and purred next to the witch's ear, causing her to shiver, "All up to you, my little witch. Porta here is not only a master chef, but has the magical prowess to create whatever your witchy heart desires."

Meg looked at Porta and said, "In that case, make me the creamiest and cheesiest Mac and Cheese."

"Of all the food in the world, why choose that," Mia asked.

The witch turned her head to face the shifter, who was still leaning next to her face, "Comfort food. I think I'm entitled to that after what I went through a few days ago," Meg cheeks heated as looked back at Porta, thinking that she just asked a magical master chef for a side dish from the kid's menu, "I don't feel like fighting with a lot of food on a plate and-"

"Say no more," Porta cut her off, still smiling, "No need to justify your order. Comfort food is something that I can do easily enough," her smile dissipated into a frown as she added, "Unfortunately all the victims of the Reset need it the most right now."

"Can I also have a soda?"

Porta's smile returned, seemingly brighter than before, "What kind, child? Say it and it's yours."

"Pepsi, please."

The elderly woman looked at the shifter and asked, "Your usual or are you busy tending your witch?"

Mia chuckled as she leaned back, "Yes to both. Today has been difficult, but I'm stopping to eat before doing anything else with her."

"Good. See to it that you do," Porta answered, her voice gave Meg the impression that she was way older than she appeared. Power emanated from the old woman as she spoke, "You're no good to anyone, especially Meg here, if you don't keep up your strength. Understand?"

"Yes ma'am," the shifter answered the chef like she was a leader of the facility, which she very well could be, the witch mused. Porta weaved her hands in a quick flurry and then placed two food trays on the counter top.

Mia handed Meg her tray and her eyes widened and her belly growled loudly. Her mouth salivated as the aroma that steamed up to her nostrils hit her. She knew that this wasn't a powder cheese variety Mac and Cheese, this one had various cheeses and looked so creamy that, if it were possible, she'd swim in it. Meg teared up as she smiled and said, "Thanks."

"No problem. If anyone gives you shit about what you put in your body," Porta answered with a wink, "you send them to me and I'll deal with them most harshly on your behalf."

The wheelchair moved away from the counter, towards the side door that led to the terrace. Meg tried to restrain a squeal of delight, but failed. She could tell that the shifter had her tray balanced on the handles, so the witch kept her movements to a minimum.

Mia turned the wheelchair around, using her butt to open the door and pull the witch outside. Meg was assailed by the floral scent of the different varieties of flowers and the distinct smell of rain that was drizzling down on them. Mia swiftly turned around and trotted over to the nearest table under the pergola.

Meg placed her tray on the table and stood up to sit on the cushion bench seat. It was softer than she expected but a little damp but it didn't bother her. The witch lived in the Pacific Northwest all her life, so rain never troubled her. Mia moved the wheelchair out of the way and sat her tray and herself down opposite of the witch.

She saw Meg gazing at her plate and defensively snapped, "What are you staring at. I love meat and the bloodier the better!"

"Sorry. I was just trying to figure out what it was. I have a big bowl of Mac and Cheese. It's not like I have any room to criticize."

"This doesn't bother you at all," the shifter asked, narrowing her eyes slightly.

"No. I once had a job in a butcher shop. At the time, I had a boyfriend that loved bloody rare steaks. It made it easy to cook them for him. Kiss one side, turn, and repeat. I prefer a little longer cook on mine."

The shifter relaxed as she cut into her food and ate. She glanced at the witch as she chewed and said, "If you worked in a butcher shop, how is it that you don't recognize this?"

The witch sheepishly grins, "I wasn't that good at remembering. I was there because I was dating the owner's son. I was used as a pretty face for the front of the store. I saw the cuts of meat, but I used cheat cards behind the counter to help me remember, but most people pointed at what they wanted."

"And nothing stuck?"

"I never said that I was a good employee. When I broke up with the owner's son, I quit as well. For some reason, information when working on a job like that never was retained. I guess that could explain why I'm a terrible witch and person in general."

"Don't say that about yourself," the shifter replied, fiercely glaring, "You may not know how to retain certain things, but that doesn't make you a terrible person, let alone a terrible witch."

Meg looked down at her food. She shrugged her shoulders as she stirred her spoon and replied, "You pretty much accused me of being a terrible witch. If you think I am, then it must be true."

Meg put a heaping spoonful into her mouth and her eyes rolled back. *Heavenly*, the witch gushed mentally as she slowly savored the creamiest Mac and Cheese she ever had. Every aspect of the dish was perfect. Whatever recipe Porta used must be a well-kept secret.

Mia's lips parted, "I didn't mean for you to take it that way, Meg. Honestly."

The witch ate more of her food and said between bites, "No, you were spot on about everything. I have my gifts as a witch, but the idea that they can affect the physical world seems preposterous, yet I can't ignore what I've seen so far." She eyed the shifter and added, "I may not be any help here."

"With the guidance and proper training, I'm sure you will surprise everyone, including yourself."

Chapter Eleven

Meg smiled and nodded. They both sat silently finishing their entrees. As she drank her Pepsi, Mia said, "Flank."

"Beg pardon?"

"The cut of meat I ate is a flank steak."

"Oh," Meg smiled as she stood up. She downed the last of her soda and walked over to the wheelchair. She sat down with her tray on her lap as Mia grasped the handles and pushed her forward towards the other side of the terrace.

The shifter stopped to open the door and grabbed Meg's tray. She placed both their trays on a well-worn counter, next to several other piles of dirty dishes and cutlery. As the shifter came back to shove the wheelchair back into the facility, the witch wondered who was in charge of cleaning the dishes. She got her answer as a strange looking being appeared.

Its skin was shiny and fluorescent. The creature had three stumpy legs and three tentacles with some wicked looking barbs, all attached to its bulbous body that consisted of a large maw with razor sharp teeth and numerous little eyes. It seemed delighted, at least that's the feeling that Meg got as it snaked it slimy tongue over the dirty dishes.

The witch looked up at the shifter as they rounded the corner, out of view of the strange entity, and asked, "I know that you know that I'm ignorant about a lot of things, so could you please tell me what that creature was back there?"

"Otyugh," Mia smiled down at the witch, "That's what they are called. They eat garbage and rummage through it looking for 'treasures'. We have a few here but they tend to keep to themselves. It saves us from using a trash company, but don't be fooled. Otyugh can and will fight, if need be, and you don't want to be on the business end of those tentacles or that mouth."

Meg shivered at the thought of being eaten alive by one. It was bad enough that she already experienced it first hand with the Ferals. Further down the corridor, the sounds of grunting and metal clanking against metal echoed from both sides. They came upon walls that had thick, shatter-proof plexiglass. The witch saw people sparring and different kinds of creatures wrestling on her right.

The other side, different groups paired together and were fighting with an assortment of melee weapons. Further down in the room, individuals trained with both crossbows and longbows.

"If you didn't guess already," Mia spoke as they strolled by, "these are the training rooms. I plan on training you here so that you can protect yourself better."

"Why would I need that? Are we going to war or something?"

"Yes," Mia replied somberly, "and not just with the Ferals. They're but a symptom of the Reset. Other beings are coming to take over our world so we all need to be prepared to fight. With weapons, magic, or fists. Whether you like it or not, you're a part of this battle."

The witch nodded and asked, "Will I be taught proper magic here?"

They turned the corner and went up a steep incline that led to the upper level of the facility.

Just how big is this place?

Mia grunted as she pushed harder, trying to make it to the level floor. Meg could hear her panting from exertion and it made her feel guilty. As they finally crested to the top, Eric hovered there, shaking his head.

"It's about time you made it here..."

Meg flipped him off as the shifter growled at the ghost, "Piss off, ghost boy. Mia is doing the best that she can with this little wreck before you. Why must you hang around?"

"You are my burden to bear...The Protector deems this necessary...To guide you..." The ghost answered with a defeated tone.

"Guide me? Guide me with what?"

"How should I know...I wasn't made privy to this information..."

"She needs to heal and prepare for war," Mia snapped as she rushed through the ghost, causing her and the witch to shiver.

"Very mature of you, mutt..." Eric growled as he flew next to the wheelchair, glaring spectral daggers at Mia, *"I never asked for this kind of afterlife...To be saddle to an ignorant, moody witch...Who in their right mind would want that...?"*

The shifter yanked the wheelchair to an abrupt halt, causing Meg to grasp the side handles. The shifter leaned down and wrapped her arms around Meg's chest possessively as she coldly retorted, "Label me crazy then. I have no issue being with Meg. She may not understand everything that's happening, but I *will* be supportive and teach her. If you have nothing better to do than talk down to her, I suggest that you find the nearest bathroom and flush your negative ass down the toilet!"

"Hmph...Obviously from the glazed look and confused expression on her face... You haven't told her everything..." The ghost sneered as it said

before disappearing, "*Good luck on how that turns out for you, Mia...*"

The shifter growled but still clung to the witch. Meg wanted to know more and knew that Mia was keeping something from her. She reached up to touch her arms, but Mia let go and stomped forward as she pushed the wheelchair.

"Why you were entrusted with *that* ghost, I'll never know."

Meg remained silent. She could feel the intense anger rolling off the shifter and didn't want to add to it because she had a bad habit of speaking without thinking. This wolf has teeth and claws, something that the witch didn't want to go up against and yet, she couldn't help seeing the beauty in her beast.

"Your ghost boy is one syllable away from uttering his last."

"He's been around me long enough that I know what he says is true. Why won't you accept it?"

They stopped beside a green door that a young redheaded woman stood next to as Mia answered, "Maybe so, but in my eyes and my heart, I see you in an entirely different perspective. This is your quarters and this is Barbara. She's going to guard your door, just in case Axel manages to get by the twins."

"Ah, Meg!" The redhead beamed a loving smile, "It's good to see you up and around."

"Do I know you?" The witch asked, squinting as she tried to place her.

"No but I was with the team that brought you here. I actually drove your SUV with you and Mia in the back. It's a little banged up but it works fine."

"Does that mean that you're a shifter too?"

Barbara nodded, still smiling, "Panther. If anyone tries to disturb you, I will turn them into my personal scratching post."

Meg smiled and nodded as she stood up, the witch had a feeling that she was going to like the redhead. Barbara opened the door for them and then resumed her guard position. Mia turned on the light as the witch wandered inside. She gasped as she asked, "This is all for me? For real?"

The room was spacious, probably five hundred square feet Meg estimated. It had a TV along with a small mini fridge. Drapery colorfully accented the monochromatic concrete walls. There were two other doors. One led to a private bathroom and the other was a reach-in closet that had all of the witch's possessions in it.

A queen size bed was the eye-catching piece of the room. It had a poofy duvet that had the image of a forest, half a dozen pillows piled by the headboard that appeared hand-carved recently. Meg couldn't help walk over, pull back the duvet, and jump on the bed with a giggle. It was both soft as a cloud and smooth as silk, which was exactly what the sheets underneath her was.

Meg smiled contently with her eyes closed, feeling the heavy pull of comfortable sleep that awaited her. A shift on the mattress beside her and an arm draped across her chest let her know that the shifter was still here.

She felt her hot breath tantalizing her ear, "Yes," Mia purred next to the witch's ear, causing her to blush, "Nothing is too good for *my* witch."

Meg nibbled on her bottom lip nervously as she asked, "Um...Mia? I have a question for you?"

"Ask away, I will answer it if I can."

"More than once I've heard others refer to me as '*your witch*'. You just said it now. Am I missing something here? Am I your *pet* to your race?"

Silence was the immediate answer, which made the witch open her eyes and look at Mia. The shifter kept averting her eyes, her hands tactical on the silk sheet.

Is she nervous? Should I be?

Mia gulped slightly when she spoke with a nervous laugh, "No. You're not a pet, but you *are* mine."

Meg snorted, "Thanks for being vague. That cleared it all up for me. Start talking, wolf. What's going on?"

The shifter's eyes changed, taking on her wolf traits. Meg shifted uncomfortably away, but Mia pulled her back, "I'm not sure that you're ready to hear it or not. Your ignorance of the Reset has left many questions for you. I was privy to some of the things that were to occur."

"But why are you afraid to tell?"

Mia let out a low growl, "I'm *not* afraid! The issue is, how will you react to this knowledge."

The witch placed her hands on Mia's face, causing her eyes to shift back to normal, "You won't know until you actually tell me, so spill it. I'm a big girl, I can take it."

"Fine, but so help me if you start freaking out, I'll smack you. Trust me, I don't want to do that." Meg smirk as she emulated the motion of zipping her mouth shut and then handed the imaginary key to her.

"I have to give this some context because the short and sweet answer won't work here. As you may or may not know, the Reset is a way of culling a society when it gets so

175

advanced technologically that nature is no longer connected to it. This has happened a few times in Earth's history, though humanity never knew it. This Reset isn't like all the other ones. This one is on a global scale."

"Humanity is about to lose a great deal of its population, but it was going to be a lot worse than that. From what I've been told, the different governments around the world devised a plan to kill off the elderly and the sick, using different strains of the influenza virus, each one becoming more deadly than the last. These agents of chaos actually summoned a deity and had Him use his magic to help boost the chances of success."

Meg listened intently but asked, "What does any of this matter and how is it related to my question?"

"Patience, my little witch," Mia stated, caressing her cheek, "I'll get to it if you can refrain from asking questions."

The witch nodded, enjoying the shifter's tender touch, as Mia continued, "The deity they summoned used the human's viruses as a way to save lives by tweaking it magically, but at the same time, made it a lot worse. The Protector is actually the one that summoned him while she was still human. He gave her a choice and with it, made humans that have gifts immune to the viruses. Those that didn't receive this protection either became what we call the Blissful Victims or the Ferals. The idea was that when these two groups died off, those with the gifts would care for the Earth and be better in tune with nature."

Mia shifted uncomfortably, "Now I'm going to answer your question. With all the chaos and turmoil caused by this Reset, the veil on this world has crumbled and interdimensional rifts have been cropped up everywhere. For this reason, the Protector asked entities to come here and help protect and guide the survivors. She enticed us with the notion that we may find...someone special."

As the shifter's cheeks redden, Meg cautiously spoke, "I think I know where this is going. I've read enough paranormal romance novels. Are you talking about life mates?"

"Something like that. Some may find love or companionship. It depends upon the race because each one is different. I've saved plenty of lives and lost so much more that I was about to give up hope, until I found you once again, Meg."

The witch's eyes widened as she sat up with her back against the headboard and incredulously gasped, "You think I'm the one for you? You sure about it because I'm not the settle down kind of girl. I'm moody as hell and I'm a royal pain in ass to be around." She sighed as she added, hanging her head, "You might be in for the disappointment of a lifetime, if you want to be with me."

Mia's lips parted slightly, then she snapped them closed quickly. She reached out and gently squeezed Meg's leg, just below her knee.

"See? This is why I didn't just blurt it out. I wanted you to know the reason behind it, so that you can think about it. Whether we're friends or something more than that, I'm willing to try. I only ask that you consider it."

The shifter stood up and pulled both the sheet and duvet over the witch's legs. She leaned in and pressed her soft lips firmly against Meg's forehead for a good five seconds. The witch couldn't resist deeply inhaling Mia's scent. She wanted to pull her into the bed with her and snuggle, but the shifter pulled away.

She walked towards the door but before she left, Mia said, "Rest well, my little witch. I've got another rescue run to go on tonight. In the morning, your training begins."

Mia turned off the light and closed the door behind her just as Meg grumpily muttered, "Oh fun."

Chapter Twelve

"Wake up, witch..." Eric said as he hovered next to the bed.

Meg weakly grumbled, "No. Come back next year."

"You're snoring loud enough to wake up the dead..."

"I don't snore," the witch bristled defensively.

"My apologies...," the ghost replied sarcastically, *"It must have been that banshee that haunts this room...It couldn't possibly be coming from you..."*

Meg sat up and growled as she threw a pillow through the ghost, "Piss off, ghost boy!" The witch slipped off the bed and shuffle-stomped towards the bathroom. Her body still ached, but the sleep helped her feel better, she thought to herself as she did her business.

"When you finish creating your witch's poo, you're to head to the training room..."

The witch hissed, "Damn it, can't a girl get a little privacy? Get out!"

"Hmph..." Eric huffed as he hovered next to her, *"You act as though I haven't seen you naked..."*

"Maybe so, but since this shit storm hit, I haven't had any alone time. I need time to think."

The ghost nodded as he moved away and slowly dissipated. Meg jabbed her fingers through her hair and grasped her head. She slowly breathed, trying to relax.

Why can't they just let me rest?

The witch groaned as she wiped and flushed the toilet. She stood up and went to wash her hands and got a good look at herself in the mirror. She felt her body vibrating. It didn't concern her since it didn't hurt. It just felt strange. The witch half frowned as she spoke, "I look like a grilled crap sandwich and that shifter still wants to be with me? What a joke."

She scrubbed her hands with a bar of soap and then splashed water on her face. Meg was going to be training so what's the point of make-up or looking good.

"I'm not a morning witch. This is what you get," Meg muttered as she stepped out of the bathroom. She went to the closet and pulled out form fitting Cami top and sweatpants, as well as her calf high leather boots. As she dressed, her thoughts went to the shifter. *Would Mia be waiting for me*, the witch wondered?

What training did she have planned for her? Meg rolled her shoulders several times before she stood up and walked out of her room. She was greeted by Barbara, who had two Styrofoam cups in her hands. She smiled as she handed one to the witch. She sniffed it and immediately took a sip of the hot, black coffee. She smiled as it warmed her up, knowing that it matched the color of her soul.

"Thanks, but how did you know I like my coffee black?"

"I didn't," Barbara winked as she pulled out little packets of sugar and creamer, "That's why I brought these, just in case. Come, I'll escort you to the training room."

The thick leather soles of the witch's boots clacked on the cold, concrete floor, echoing eerily, and yet Barbara's footwear made no sound at all.

They walked silently in tandem down the steep sloped floor. Meg glanced over at the shifter several times, noticing that she kept eyeing her, smiling.

Meg stopped just as they reached the lower level floor and asked, "Why do you keep smiling at me? Am I amusing to look at? I'm not a morning person so don't judge my looks."

Barbara slowly sipped her coffee as her eyes glowed, her feline traits showing, "I'm smiling because you give me a glimmer of hope." The shifter turned and trotted forward. The witch rushed to keep up, but the shifter seemed to glide faster along the floor with ease.

Panting, Meg shouted, "What do you mean by that? How did I give you hope? I've done nothing, other than being a play toy for Ferals and an ignorant, invalid here."

Barbara opened the door and let Meg enter the training room. It looked like an old gymnasium with thick blue padding covering the entire floor, the smell of body odor, sweat, and blood permeated the air. There were several punching bags at one end of the room near a rack of dumbbells and free weights. Rows of bullseye targets lined the opposite end attached to stacks of hay. Meg heard the click of a button and the hum of mechanical parts filled the air.

The witch watched as an apparatus unfolded from the wall before them. As it stretched and shifted into place, it resembled a small obstacle course. Meg turned around to ask Barbara about it but paused. The woman had stripped all her clothes off and placed them folded neatly on the floor.

"Are you my trainer today?" Meg asked, feeling a bit awkward, "If so, I think I'm wearing the wrong attire for this."

Barbara laughed as she approached her, "No, my dear. I'm going to shift and use that obstacle course over there. It keeps the animal in me happy if it can run." The shifter pointed at a gray door by the archery range, "Your trainer is behind that door over there."

Barbara seamlessly shifted before Meg's eyes, causing her mouth to hang open. Before her stood a panther with crimson fur.

"God's, you're magnificent and beautiful,"

"A pretty kitten isn't always the best choice for protection," a masculine voice spoke, one that Meg recognized immediately. Meg turned and saw the towering, mass that was Axel. He glared at the witch with disdain as he approached.

The panther swiftly moved in between the two, letting out a protective growl.

"Did the boy live?" Meg asked, wanting to know if she would be constantly on the watch for Axel.

He sneered as he replied, "Why do you care? He's dead and yet, you survived. I don't think it's fair that it went that way. Let's spar, you pathetic little witch and let's see what you're made of. I'll allow you to use your magic on me, how does that sound?"

"I don't know any magic," Meg tore her gaze away from Axel's predatory glare for a moment, but then she looked back at him, chin

185

jutted out defiantly as her body tensed to the point that the vibrating grew painful, "If you feel the need to toss me around like a ragdoll, then do it. I refuse to stay here and constantly worry about you killing me in my sleep!"

"That's a lie and you know it!" Axel hissed, "You're thrumming with magic as we speak. Unleash your worst on me, I don't fear you, witch!"

Barbara lunged at Axel, swiping her deadly claws at him. He dodged each strike, despite having his scowling eyes locked on the witch. Meg watched as he blocked the panther's muscular limbs and threw a brain jarring right hook, sending Barbara flying. The massive cat toppled over several times before lying on the mats, barely moving. Axel glowered at the panther as he mocked, "Be a good kitty and stay down."

Meg snarled as she charged at Axel. He was caught by surprise as she landed several body blows. He grunted as each one connected as the witch roared, "You leave her alone, you big bully! If you think I'm going to stand by and watch you hurt her, then you're as dim as you're thick! Just kill me and get over with already! C'mon, fight back!"

Axel backpedaled as Meg continued her onslaught, his scowl was gone as his face revealed flashes of pain and surprise. He growled as he threw a right hook, aiming for the witch's temple, but Meg managed to surprise him again. She dropped down, doing the splits, and slammed her fists into his groin.

Axel dropped down to his knees, clutching his crotch as tears streamed down his chiseled face. He painfully whined, "Bad form! You hit me below the belt!"

"Like you wouldn't do it," Meg retorted as she jumped to her feet, delivering an uppercut that toppled the giant onto his back. The witch rushed over to Barbara, who shifted back into her human form. She kneeled beside the woman and frantically asked, "Barbara, are you okay? Speak to me?"

"Just a little woozy. Axel hits like a wrecking ball. I don't recommend getting on his bad side."

"I think it's a little late for that," Meg nervously chuckled. Barbara glanced over at the big man and couldn't believe her bleary eyes. He was down on the floor, groaning in pain as he clutched his crotch and midsection.

A slow, dramatic clapping drew their attention. Meg helped the stunned shifter to her feet, supporting her weight as a small, humanoid being approached. It was probably two and a half feet tall and had wrinkly green skin and no hair anywhere. Its hands and feet had four digits with marble white claws at the ends. The rest of its body was covered with a gray, skin-tight bodysuit. It beamed a genuine smile, which caused the witch's anger to ebb.

"I'm sorry I failed to protect you, Meg," Barbara hung her head in shame as she let go of the witch.

"Don't worry about it. Axel picked the wrong bitch to mess with."

"You don't fight fair!" Axel groaned from his prone position.

"Do you want more, buddy?" Meg growled as she stomped towards the downed shifter, "Get up so I can knock you down again! You will *not* be threatening me, ever again, or do I need to beat it into you some more?"

Axel held his arms and hands up protectively, "You used some nasty magic on me, bitch!"

"From what I heard you say earlier, you told her to use it against you, Axel." The tiny being replied with a knowing gaze.

"Not dark magic," Axel whined as Barbara and the small humanoid being hovered over him. The diminutive creature placed his hand on Axel's shoulder and it caused it to recoil its hand.

"I told you. Dark magic. Tell her to take it back, Adoy!"

The creature replied, "There's no such thing as dark magic. Magic is pure energy. The only darkness is what resides in the user and their intent." Adoy turned his head, scrutinizing the witch with its intense stare. "That said, what was your intent?"

"What do you mean? Isn't it obvious? I wanted to beat his sorry ass for threatening me. I lost it when he hurt her! I can't stand bullies, never have and never will."

Adoy walked over to the witch. He reached his small hand and grasped her hand and asked, "What is your best magical talent or are we seeing it on display over there?"

Meg smirked, "I can finish three bottles of wine in less than five minutes."

Adoy blinked. He eyed her, "I'm being serious."

"So am I," Meg replied as she sheepishly scratched her arm, "I've casted karma spells and created blessed water in a salt circle, but beyond that, I have zero talent like the rest of you people here"

"If that's true," Adoy pointed at Axel, "then how did you manage that spell?"

"What spell?" Meg asked, feeling confused, "All I did was beat up a bully. What's the big deal?"

Axel cried in agony, pleading, "Meg, I beg you! Take your curse off me, please. It hurts!"

"You should've thought about it before you tried to hurt me and my new friend," Meg hissed as she stormed over to him. She glowered down at him menacingly, but her rage wavered as she saw the results of her attack.

"I can remove it, but," Adoy looked up at the witch, "it would be easier if she did it. Remove your magic from this man."

"How can I when I don't know what I did in the first place?" The witch growled at the entity.

"Don't get snippy with me, Meg," Adoy commanded, all his calm vanished. "You *will* show me the respect that I deserve."

"She's an ignorant witch," Barbara stated, "Meg needs your help learning how to use her natural gifts, Adoy. Can you guide her on how to do it?"

Meg glared at the shifter, but knew she was correct. Adoy tapped his white clawed finger against his round chin, contemplating what to do. Axel cried out as he clenched his jaw, his fists were balled up. He pointed at the mammoth shifter's side and commanded, "Sit. Your first lesson begins now."

Meg complied as she sat cross-legged by Axel. He looked at her through teary eyes, "I'm sorry, Meg."

"Next time, don't threaten me," the witch hissed.

Adoy put his tiny hand on her shoulder and admonished, "Enough of that. It's time to heal, not attack."

Meg nodded, as she released a breath of frustration, "What do I do to remove it?"

"Place your hands on him," Adoy stated, taking on the role of a teacher, "Open your mind's eye and look at the energy that you pushed into poor Axel here."

Meg thought better about a sarcastic comment that she wanted to say and focused on her breathing. As she fell into a meditative state with her eyes closed, she looked at Axel and gasped. He was covered in a black energy that looked like it was shocking him with an electrical current.

"I'm so sorry, Axel," Meg grimaced as she felt the pain the magic caused, "How do I help him? I'm not sure if I can."

"If you can attack, then you can heal. Magic is neither good nor evil, just gray and pure. It will obey your commands, your intent. At this point, you can either make Axel experience more pain and suffering or call it back into you. If you take it in yourself, you *will* feel the pain. That said, what will you do?"

Meg thought about it. She didn't want to leave it in Axel, but at the same time, she didn't want it in her either.

"If this magic obeys me, can I push it into the Earth?"

"It would be the best course of action, witch," Adoy smiled as he added, "but you'll need to decide what happens to it when you do this. If not, it could go bad, really quick."

Meg nodded as she asked, "So, how do I call it to me?"

"Focus on it and call it back to you, verbally or mentally. Your intent is everything, so be sure you mean it."

"You can do it, Meg!" Barbara piped up, cheering on the witch.

Meg smiled to herself. She managed to focus on her magic and mentally called out, *"Come back to me, now."*

The magic quickly shifted from Axel to Meg's body. The raw power coursed swiftly through her like water flooding out from a dam. The witch fell over and curled up in a ball, screaming, "Oh Gods, it hurts!"

"Yes, it does," Adoy stated calmly, "As I said, you need to be specific about what you want to do with it. You have it, now push it into the Earth. Concentrate and do it before it burns out your synapses."

The witch gritted her teeth as she tried catching her breath. It was difficult to focus from the excruciating pain, but she mentally commanded, *"Move to the Earth, damnit!"*

"It doesn't look like it's working," Axel said as he sat, watching intently.

"I think I know the problem. Axel, sit her up." Adoy barked.

Axel hesitantly touched her; he could feel the power thrumming within her. Barbara sat down next to the witch and supported her left side. Adoy put his hand on Meg's head and told her, "You should've grounded yourself before doing this."

"Sorry," Meg bit out, "Forgot!"

Adoy grumbled, "I should have said it, but I figured that you would've done it first. Allow me to do it, then push it out and make sure and say your command *three* times."

Meg felt like a novice as she felt roots extend from her tailbone. *The magical teacher was right, I should've grounded from the start*, she berated herself. As her roots delved deeper into the ground, Meg commanded the magic to disperse in the Earth.

"Go into the Earth to be cleansed and purified for later use...Go into the Earth to be cleansed and purified for later use...Go into the Earth to be cleansed and purified for later use..."

The magic flushed down her winding roots slowly but steady, much to Meg's relief. She felt hands rubbing her back. She glanced over her shoulder and smiled at the redheaded shifter. Then she glanced at Axel, who was doing the same thing. The witch glared at him but it didn't deter him, "You have nothing to fear from me, Meg."

"Why? Because I beat your ass?"

"No," Axel looked away, "it was wrong of me to blame you for *my* own issues with the whole Reset."

"Are you looking for forgiveness? If you are, I'm fresh out buddy!"

"I deserve your ire and malice, just don't use that nasty magic on me again. I will endeavor to win your trust," he glanced at the witch with a lopsided grin, "I'm certain that will take me several life times."

"True," Meg smirk, "but gifts and groveling are a good start."

"Meg," Adoy spoke calmly, "unground and follow me. Your training has just begun."

"This should count towards that, right?" Meg said.

"If anything, it just reinforces the need for proper training, witch. Follow me."

The witch huffed as she stood up but got yanked back down on her ass. "What the - oh, right." Meg rolled her eyes as her cheeks heated up under the scrutinizing eyes of the magic teacher. She ungrounded herself by pulling the roots back inside her. Meg stood up and followed Adoy across the training room, towards the gray door.

Chapter Thirteen

Meg wasn't sure exactly how much time had passed during her time with Adoy, but all the muscles in her body were screaming for respite. He called it *'a crash course in magical knowledge and skills'*, the witch felt drained both mentally and magically.

Now I know how Luke Skywalker felt during his time at Dagobah.

Meg giggled to herself as she shuffled down the long corridor. Her trainer reminded her of the little green Jedi Master in the swamp. She just now realized this, the entire time during training, her brain kept on nagging her that she knew the little creature. The witch looked up at the inclined walkway and sighed.

Why can't I fly on a damn broom?

Meg shook her head as she grasped the rail on the wall. Adoy was a creature of pure magic, she learned, and could be anywhere he wanted with a thought. *He could've taken me back to my room,* Meg grumbled mentally. She felt a hand on her shoulder, which startled her because whomever it was didn't make a sound.

Meg turned quickly, her hands clenched and pulsating with magic.

"Settled down, witch," Victor calmly said as he removed his hand, "I see your training is coming along nicely."

"Next time, announce yourself!" Meg hissed.

"It's who I am," the vampire flashed his fangs, "Stealth and death. I can't turn it off, you know."

"You can clear your throat or something."

"This I know, but I choose not to."

Meg labored her way up the incline, glaring at the vampire as he followed by her side effortlessly.

"Why are you bothering me," Meg huffed out, "Don't you have a neck to bite elsewhere?"

"Are you offering," Victor grinned mischievously, "I never turn down an invitation like that."

"I'm being serious."

"So was I." Victor smiled but then it waned, concern etched into his face, "You should be resting. You look like you're about to collapse."

Meg rolled her eyes, "I'm fine. I'm going to my room. Yoda put me through a lot."

"Yoda?" The vampire said, confusion clouded his eyes, "There's no one here by that name." Meg laughed, which irritated him, "What's so damn amusing?"

"You haven't been to the movies in a while, have you?"

"No. I prefer books to those silly moving pictures." Victor replied as he raised his head snobbishly, "I never saw the point when you can have an adventure all on your own, in your mind."

"You never said why you're here?"

Victor smirked, "No, I didn't."

Meg stopped and looked at the vampire, "I'm in no mood for games. State your business and move on."

"Child, you don't scare me. I'm not Axel," his eyes pinned the witch in place. She held her breath as he leaned down into her personal space, "I'm here to escort you to an important meeting. Nothing more, unless you say otherwise."

"What kind of meeting?" Meg barely squeaked out; her throat parched.

"One that we're both late for. Come, child."

"A snail's pace is my current top speed," Meg answered as she turned and walked forward. The vampire sighed and before the witch knew what was happening, he picked her up and threw her over his shoulder.

"Hey!" Meg cried out as she smacked Victor's back, "Put me down, damnit!"

The halls and everything around them blurred as the vampire ran through the facility. Meg closed her eyes as nausea churned in her stomach.

"Don't puke on me," Victor warned, "The suit is expensive and imported, so spew away from it."

"Slow down and I'll spare your vanity the squishy contents of my tummy," the witch retorted as they came to a sudden halt. Victor opened a door as he sat Meg down, her feet firmly planted on the floor. She turned and saw a spacious conference room filled with a plethora of entities, some looked human while others appeared to be otherworldly. There was a huge surveillance system on the far wall, each screen showed different areas of Portland and other cities.

"Thanks for bringing her here, Victor," Mia stated as she protectively escorted Meg into the room.

"Careful," the vampire quipped with a smile, "this one is ready to spew like a water fountain."

"Piss off, fang boy!" Meg sneered as she stuck her tongue out at him. A petite woman with a long flowing red dress tapped on the side of her tumbler with a spoon, getting everyone's attention. She looked human, for the most part, except for her eyes. They were forest green and glowing...

"I see that we have a few new faces with us," the woman stared at Meg, causing her to feel uncomfortable. "Our other teams have reported that more will be arriving shortly. Night is almost upon us, Victor? Is your team ready for tonight's hunt?"

"Just waiting for the pesky sun to go down for some of the newer members of our squad."

"Very well," the woman locked her gaze on Mia, "Raids by your pack have brought about new life in this dreary place. You are to be commended for your efforts."

Mia bowed her head, "We weren't able to save everyone," she glanced at Axel sympathetically.

"Losses are to be expected and in great numbers at this point in time. The more people we can bring here, the better because war is coming. We need to be prepped and ready. Meg?"

"Yes?" the witch gulped, but felt the shifter squeeze her hand.

"I'm going to need you to aid Master Adoy in the coming weeks. I know you are severely lacking, but you will get better and may learn more from the others that arrive."

"I will try," she glanced at Mia and then asked, "Will I be going out on any raids?"

"Eventually, yes. It's necessary to send out diverse teams, but we can't at the moment. We can only do so much with what precious life we have here. Some of the Fae are returning from the far south shortly. Hopefully, with good news. If not, please have the medical bay prepped and ready to receive the wounded, doctor."

"Yes, Gaylish!" A small group, including Dr Arnica moved swiftly out of the room. Meg felt overwhelmed and completely out of her league amongst these supernatural beings. Gaylish surveyed the room and asked, "Are there any questions? If not, go back to what you were doing. That is all. Meg, step forward."

As creatures funneled out of the room, Meg slowly made her way to the leader with Mia at her side. As she drew near, the witch could feel the power emanating from Gaylish. Whatever she was, Meg knew that it would be wise not to get on her bad side.

"It's good to see you up and around, witch," Gaylish purred as she circled the two women, "I'm hoping that you're feeling welcome and adjusting to this new reality."

"It's a lot to process but I'll make it."

"Is it true that you used dark magic on Axel today," Gaylish stopped in front of the witch, eyeing her.

Meg shifted from foot to foot nervously. She looked down at the floor, but Gaylish pulled her head up by her chin. "Don't fear me, *little witch*. Just tell me what occurred."

"Axel was being a dick. He hurt Barbara and I couldn't handle seeing him hurting her, so I attacked him with my fists. I didn't realize that I was using magic on him, let alone dark magic. Honestly, I swear!"

Gaylish let go of Meg's chin, chuckling as she did, "I'm sure that it felt good. Felt right, didn't it?"

"I don't like bullies. If I have to, I will stand up to all of them here. I'm barely recovering and he threatened to kill me? I don't think so!"

"That's the kind of spirit that I hoped you would bring in here," Gaylish smiled proudly and then turned her steely gaze upon the shifter, "I'd say that you need to put him in his place, but Meg seems to have done it for you."

Mia's cheeks heated slightly, "I'll make it a point to have a little chat with him. You have my word."

"If he doesn't see reason," Gaylish smirked as she pointed at the witch, "you can threaten him by having your witch intervene."

"You're not mad at what I did?" Meg gasped.

"No, but I do expect you to have a better understanding and control of your magic. Is that clear?"

"Crystal."

Gaylish curtly nodded, "Good. Off you go."

Mia snaked her arm around Meg's waist and escorted her out of the room, leaving Gaylish to watch the different monitors. The witch wasn't sure where they were, but the shifter led the way, still holding onto her. Meg breathed deeply, inhaling Mia's scent and smiling. She heard the sound of a wrapper being crinkled.

"Take it, Meg. It's a chocolate protein bar. I can tell that you need the energy."

"Thanks," Meg smiled as she graciously accepted the food. She bit into it and before she realized it, she had finished it off. They came to an abrupt stop in the corridor by a brown door. Mia opened the door and asked, "Care to come in and relax?"

"Sure, but where are we at? I'm lost."

Mia smiled coyly, "This is my room. The door's always open to you."

Chapter Fourteen

Meg stepped inside and her senses were assailed by Mia's scent but also the damp air that reminded the witch of the forest. Mia's walls were adorned with weapons of various kinds. There was a queen size bed with a simple blanket and pillows, but what caught Meg's attention was one picture on the nightstand.

A picture of Meg dancing around a bonfire in the country.

She looked over at the shifter, who shrugged her shoulders, "I found your address in your glove compartment. I wanted something that I could look at. A picture of happier times."

The witch sat down on the side of the bed and picked up the picture. She lightly ran her fingertips over her image and sighed, "Happier times, long gone by." She looked at the shifter and asked, "Of all the pictures of me in my house, why pick this one?"

Mia sat down beside her, leaning her warm body against the witch, "You look so full of life and happy. I hope to see you like that once again."

"Will there be better times or is this going to be the new normal?"

"The world is changing, that much is obvious," the shifter replied as she nuzzled against Meg's neck, causing her to moan softly, "the Reset is temporary and violent but it will pass. I don't know when it will end, but there's more at play."

Meg looked at Mia, concern etched into her face, "How can it get worse?"

"The veil of this world has fallen, which means there will be rifts opening all over the world. These holes lead to other dimensions, some good and bad. This is why we are building an army. To fight for this world and," Mia brushed hair away from Meg's ear and kissed it, making the witch shiver, "protect the ones that we care about the most."

"But you don't even know me. I'm a terrible person who has a relationship track record of bad decisions." Meg sighed as her shoulders slumped, "You would be better off with someone else."

"Oh, I do know you, Meg. I've been around for a while and I've watched you from afar. I took out threats that you never knew were around you when I was more otherworldly than I am now. I've seen those bad choices in both men and women. I wanted to rip out the throats of those that caused you pain, but I couldn't. But when I got word of the Reset, I knew that I had to be with you when it happened. I'm sorry that I wasn't there to protect you from the Ferals."

"I was doing fine, as you saw from the dead bodies in my house, until I got overwhelmed by them in my car."

"I should've been there with you. I wasn't allowed to be your messenger, like Eric. Many times, I tried contacting you in your dreams or when you passed out from too much wine, but you never could hear me."

Meg thought about it, trying to recall some of her dreams. For a while, a mysterious woman had been lurking in a few of them. Always in the background and yet, she never got to speak with her. At least, not that the witch remembered.

Was Mia this mysterious lady of my dreams?

Meg laid down with her legs dangling off the side of the bed, "Who stopped you from being my messenger and why?"

"I'm not sure why, but the Protector was the one assigning entities to those with gifts." Mia answered as she laid down on her side next to her with her arm draped across the witch's chest. The shifter leaned in and pressed her lips against Meg's cheek and held it there for a few seconds.

Meg nibbled on the inside of her bottom lip, nervously waiting for more. Mia caressed her face lovingly, "You're so beautiful, Meg. I wish that you could see yourself as I see you."

The witch blushed slightly, "I'm telling you that you're going to be disappointed with me if this goes further."

The shifter rolled over and laid on top of the witch, her eyes glowed as hints of her wolf shown. Her predatory gaze made Meg feel like the main course. Mia got inches from her face, her hot breath cascading on the witch's lips as she replied, "You could *never* disappoint me, my little witch. I know you make questionable choices and this gruff front you project is how you keep others from shredding your big, beautiful heart. As I've said, I've watched you and I know what to expect from you. I'm sorry that I didn't get to know you until now."

"I'm hardly beautiful anymore," Meg replied as she cast her eyes downward, "The Ferals saw to that. I'm so messed up."

"Time heals all wounds and the scarring left in its place tells a story about how you lived and endured the pain, but it doesn't deter nor defines you as a person."

"I guess that makes me a shallow person."

Mia lifted Meg's head up with her hand under her chin, forcing her to look at her, "No. Not shallow, but a woman who's been through a lot up to this moment in time. I refuse to let anyone else hurt you, even you."

"I've got to ask." The witch spoke hesitantly, "Why haven't you kissed me yet?"

"I've wanted to kiss your sweet soft lips, but I'm unsure if you're truly ready for it. I don't want to pressure you into something that you're not ready for."

Meg sighed, "I don't have much of a choice in *that* area of my life. I'm expected to fight in a supernatural war, whether I want to or not. I'm not sure I'll ever be ready. But for you," the witch reached up and pulled the shifter down, firmly planting her lips against hers. Both Mia and Meg groaned in unison and then laughed. Meg pulled away slightly, "I'm certain that I'm ready for you, my sexy little wolf."

Mia growled as she pressed her lips against Meg's lips. She opened her mouth, trying to devour the witch, her appetite for the woman beneath her was becoming insatiable. Meg probed the shifter's mouth with her tongue, determined to show Mia that she wanted her. Mia opened her mouth and let her witch enjoy.

Meg didn't want to think about anything else. Not her training, not the Reset and all the death it's creating. Her thoughts were consumed by this wolf on top of her, her scent was both soothing and sexy. Mia kissed her way down her jawline and slowly buried her face on the witch's neck.

Meg gasped and squirmed as she ran her hands down the shifter's back, gliding down to her muscular ass. She slipped her hands under the hem of her pants and kneaded her ass roughly, making Mia growl with pleasure.

"I've waited a long time to have you all to myself. Be warned, I'm not letting you go." Mia purred.

"Now that you have me," Meg mischievously grinned, "what are you going to do with me?"

Mia growled, her voice took on an animalistic cadence, "I'm going to devour you. I will pleasure you in so many ways that you'll never want another."

The witch jutted out her chin, challenging her, "Prove it, wolf!"

Mia's eyes glowed as she raised up and pulled Meg's Cami top off. She grabbed the witch by her wrists and pinned them above her head. She bent down and gilded her tongue down Meg's neck, slowly making her way to her chest. Mia methodically stroked her tongue around one of the witch's breasts, winding up to her areola.

Meg gasped as the shifter enveloped her nipple in her mouth, lashing it with her tongue like a snake. Once her nipple hardened, Mia grazed it with her teeth and blew on it lightly. "Oh Gods! Oh damn! Please, fuck me!"

"No, I'm not done playing yet."

"But-"

"Shh, little witch," Mia put a finger on Meg's lips, sinfully smiling at her, "You challenged the wolf, so be prepared to be devoured."

Mia grinded against the witch playfully, pelvis on pelvis. Meg squirmed under the assault; her legs moved as she tried to get a release from the ever-growing arousal in her wet core. Mia shifted over to the other breast, suckling as she groped the other breast.

Meg moaned as the shifter kept teasing her. Mia caressed her bare torso, her hand gliding down to the hem of the witch's sweatpants and said, "Don't move. If you want to go further, I need to remove those lovely boots of yours."

Meg nodded quietly as Mia slinked her way between her legs. She tugged the left boot off and then the right one. The shifter rubbed Meg's feet and calves before tugging on her sweatpants. Meg lifted her hips up in the air so it would be easier for them to slide off.

The witch looked down and saw that Mia was watching her, barely peeking over her crotch. She moved in slowly, her hot breath on her core made the witch quiver with anticipation. Mia inhaled deeply, enjoying that she was the reason for Meg's arousal.

"Like I said earlier," Mia rasped, "I'm going to devour you."

"Does that make me little red riding hood in this story?" Meg grinned.

"No, because you're not a child and definitely one gorgeous woman. Now let's see how you taste, my dear," the shifter replied as she caressed her mounds with her tongue, kissing them tenderly.

Meg let a moan of pleasure escape, thinking that Mia's wicked tongue felt like the finest silk grazing her skin. Mia slid her hands under Meg's thighs and lifted her legs. She let them rest on her shoulders as she licked the witch's outer lips.

"MMM," Mia purred, "you taste exquisite, like a gift from the Gods. I can only imagine how much sweeter you are on the inside."

Mia spread the witch's core wide open and flickered her tongue over every inch, lapping up her slick sex like it was water. The shifter used her finger and thumb to massage Meg's swollen clit, causing the witch to breathe heavier. Mia paused, forcing the witch to look at her

"So," Meg panted, "why...are you...stopping...?"

"I'm savoring you," Mia replied as she licked her lips seductively before dropping her mouth over Meg's clit. She sucked on it as she lashed it with her tongue. Meg moaned louder as she squeezed her own breasts roughly, adding to her pleasure.

The shifter slipped a finger inside Meg's slick core, slowly going in and out. The witch gasped as Mia increased the speed of her finger pounding, which felt a lot faster than what she'd experienced.

"Oh Gods," Meg cried out, "Oh fuck me!"

"I am, my darling," Mia said with a giggle and then went back to stimulating her clit. Meg arched her back as she moved her pelvis in rhythm with the finger strokes. Mia pushed a second finger inside the witch's wet, swollen core, fucking her harder and faster.

"Oh damn," Meg cried out, panting hard, "I'm about...to explode!"

"Yes, my precious little witch," Mia demanded, "Explode for me, my love!"

Mia dipped her head down, licking her core as she slipped a third finger inside the witch. Meg bucked her hips as the pressure of a massive orgasm was building. Mia added a humming vibration from her mouth as she lapped up Meg's sweet nectar. The witch exploded hard; the orgasm was more intense than she expected it to. Never had she had anyone to give her a sexual pleasure of this magnitude. Meg screamed as a powerful wave of euphoria took over her senses.

Mia pulled out her fingers and spread Meg's core open. She slowly licked all the witch's sticky cum off, causing her to reflexively close her thighs on the shifter's head.

"Oh Gods...so sensitive... fuck!"

Mia managed to pry herself free from her lover's vise grip thighs and stood up. She eyed the witch as she seductively put her fingers in her mouth, sucking the sticky juices off them, "You taste way better than I expected. Definitely, the nectar of the Gods you have inside there."

Meg's breaths came in rapid and shallow. She tried to catch her breath as the room seemed to be spinning. She felt a shift of weight on the bed and saw that Mia was lying next to her, undressed.

The shifter pulled the witch into her arm and softly kissed her on the lips, "How was that, Meg? Did you enjoy it?"

"What...?" Meg replied incoherently, "What did...you say?"

"Never mind, you just answered my question." Mia purred as she held on to the witch tightly. "Maybe, if you feel up to it, you can play with me."

"I wish... I'm not sure... that I'm... able...at the moment..."

"Then let's get some sleep then. You can sleep here with me. I'm not taking no for an answer." Mia stated.

Meg half-heartedly giggled, "Like I can leave at the moment. My legs feel like Jell-O, so my ass is staying right here. Don't be surprised if I recover and take care of you with a strap on."

Mia smirked as she pointed at the closet, "There's one, along with other toys, in a plastic box in there. I won't stop you from taking full advantage of me, Meg."

Mia got up and walked over to the other side of the bed and pulled back the blanket. Meg didn't need to be told as she rolled over and let the shifter cover her sweaty body. Mia walked back to the other side as Meg pulled the blanket back for her.

"That was amazing and mind blowing! I don't think that I've ever felt a pleasurable release like that in my life."

Meg reached over as Mia slipped into the bed and cuddled with her. She inhaled her scent, reveling in the sage and cedar aroma.

"I'm glad you enjoyed it. Rest well, my love."

Chapter Fifteen

For the past six weeks, Meg had been assisting Adoy with magical training. More new faces had come in, some knew how to use their gifts, while others were severely lacking. *At least the knowledgeable ones aided with the training*, Meg thought to herself. This gave her more time to learn self-defense with weapons and hand to hand combat.

The witch learned more about her own magic. Adoy explained that it was tied to her emotions. Meg's mental state dictated what type of magic came forth, which explained why it came out as dark magic against Axel. She could wield it easily enough by touch. She didn't need a wand, but she could channel it through weapons to do more damage.

The witch looked around at the swelling class. Next to her, stood a woman that went by the name Red Jayne. She was gifted with working with energy and could use it to heal or cause harm. She came in from Salem with a young girl named Eve Driskell, who was a psychic that could read other people's thoughts. Like most people at the facility, Eve was traumatized and was a timid girl. She had her own personal demon literally to deal with.

Meg walked around the room, observing the different techniques and progress of everyone. Several Fae taught how to harness the magic in nature itself, one in particular worked exclusively with Eve.

A young man moved around, creating sigils in the air with a crimson dagger. Each one burned brightly as he directed them at some makeshift targets that could withstand magical abuse. A decent size Native American named Dan sat on the ground, meditating as a small collection of items of various sizes and weights floated around him.

Meg was astonished by the variety of gifts people had on display. Nothing seemed impossible, especially now that magic was active and manifesting everywhere. Adoy told her that it was due to the veil falling and the ley lines, that were once dormant, were now supercharged and flowing freely across the globe.

"Care to magically spar, Meg?" The young man with the crimson dagger asked as he twirled the blade.

"Sure, if you think you can keep up, Jack," the witch replied with a smile.

Jack rotated his wrist, creating a circle that flared to life. With his dagger, he channeled the magic, directing the simple sigil at the witch. Meg managed to deflect it, her own magic humming throughout her body causing her to shimmer.

Jack grinned while he conjured a triangle, an X, a square, and another circle. He released them at Meg as he recreated the same sigils again and again. He let them fly, each one striking the witch.

The sigils were absorbed by the witch's magic. She smiled and said, "Let me guess; you're a gamer, aren't you?"

"What can I say," he bowed, "I love the PlayStation so why not use the button shapes as part of my quick magic." Jack scratched his head and asked, "Did you feel them or were they too weak?"

"Button mashing at its finest. Here," Meg grinned mischievously, "let's see how you deal with a player two noob like me."

In an instant, Meg's body glowed as all the sigils burst forth like a pimple, spraying the young conjurer. He toppled over onto his back and moaned as he rubbed his chest, "Ouch...what the hell was that?"

"Your attack was fine," Meg stated as she put her hands on her hips, "It's called shielding. I simply held your attack in it and unleashed it back at you, three-fold."

"That's not nice nor was it fair," Jack grumbled as he held his hand out. Meg reached down and helped the conjurer to his feet.

"See? Your button mashing will only get you so far. Expect your opponent to be different, smarter, and tougher. Do you think that someone would stand still to let you wail on them magically?"

"I guess not," Jack had a wry smile, "How did you come up with this method?"

"I can't take credit for it," the witch hiked her thumb in the direction of Red Jayne, "Jayne schooled me when I attempted to spar with her. It was a simple but valuable lesson, one that could save your life. Bounce the attack back at the one who sent it."

"Kind of like 'I'm rubber, your glue! Whatever you say bounces off me and sticks to you!'" he smiled.

"Like I said. Simple but effective, so work on your personal shielding and protections or you will be dead before you know it, Black Jack."

"I never bust, my dear!" Jack said with pride, "That's why they call me Black Jack. I always win when the chips are down."

Mia walked in the training room in a full body, form fitting, leather attire. Meg couldn't help eye the shifter as she marched over with purpose. She nodded at Black Jack and then warmly smiled at the witch. All her emotions melted away as she announced, "We have a job to do. Get prepped, we go in twenty minutes."

Meg paled slightly, "Am I coming on this one?"

"Yes," Mia stated as she barked out, "Jack! Victor and Axel will be accompanying us downtown, they're stocking a vehicle with the necessary equipment. Get geared up, sorcerer. Meet us in the garage."

Meg bit her bottom lip, suddenly feeling the need to escape. The witch hadn't set foot outside the walls of the facility. Eric materialized beside her and stated, *"You're paler than me, witch... What's scaring you...?"*

"What're you talking about, dude," Jack asked, "Meg's a badass witch with a mean streak. Nothing scares her!" He looked at Meg and wearily added with concern, "Right, Meg?"

Before Mia could reach her, Meg bolted out of the training room, not caring if anyone was following her. She vaguely heard her name being called, but sounded hollow and distant. *Training was one thing*, the witch thought, *fighting what's beyond the walls was entirely different.*

The witch rounded the corner and collided with what felt like a brick wall. Meg looked up as she said sorry and then stopped. The creature before her had crimson and brown skin that seemed dry like leather. It wore gray cargo pants that hung low on its hip. A tattered, sleeveless biker vest and a perturbed gaze fell on the witch as it reached a clawed hand out, "Dear me, what's with the running around like a rabbit being hunted? Someone could get hurt. Here, let me-"

"I'm fine," the witch spat as she scrambled to her feet. The creature grabbed her by the arm, stopping her as Mia, Jack and Eve caught up.

"Let me go! I have something I need to do!"

"Meg, what gives?" Jack asked, feeling confused.

"Is it Axel?" Mia snarled, "Has he threatened you again?"

"No, nothing like that," Meg replied, still trying to free herself from the entity's grip.

"I swear I didn't do this to her," the crimson creature spoke, not liking how the shifter was eyeing him, "She ran into me. I'm merely trying to aid this rude lady."

"She's scared," Mia roared. she pulled the witch into her arms as the creature let go. "I'm trying to figure out what's got her all worked up."

"I'm fine," Meg growled at everyone, "Why won't you leave me alone?"

The witch felt a timid hand on her shoulder. She knew who it was without even looking, but she did. Meg's eyes were full of fear as she looked at Eve, who said, "She's afraid to go out."

"Meg ain't afraid of nothing, girl!" Black Jack answered. He pointed at the witch, "She can toss me around and bring Axel to his knees, begging for mercy. What can she possibly be afraid of.?"

Eve turned to look deadpan at the sorcerer, coldly uttered, "You know of trauma, do you?"

"Who doesn't? Everyone here's been through some shit. What does it matter?" Black Jack replied, exasperated.

The crimson creature backed away from the group, putting its hands up, "I'm no threat, Meg. Eve, speak to her please? I know you can-"

"Reach her? Be a lifeline, in her time of need? She has a *mate* that can do that for her, *demon*?" Eve hissed.

"Why are you backing away, Moneek?" Mia asked.

"Oh, Gods!" Meg cried out, trying to free herself from Mia's hold, her eyes wildly darted everywhere, "Why aren't you listening to me? Let me go!"

"She's a powerful witch, caught up in a PTSD moment," The demon replied as he moved out of Meg's view, "Do you think that I want to be her target when she's ready to fight? I'm good, thank you."

"No good demons exist," Eve muttered, knowing that Moneek could hear her. "It's her first time being told to leave this place."

Bewildered, the shifter shook her head, "What? No one told her to leave!"

"It's what she believes," Eve shrugged her shoulders.

"The mission?" Black Jack stroked his chin, "Do you think that is what caused this little freak out?"

"Did she know about it, the mission?" The psychic asked the shifter.

"No, I didn't know about the mission until ten minutes ago. Did..." Mia gulped as she held the witch against her warm body, "Are you saying that *I* caused this?"

Eve backed away as the shifter's eyes glowed, "Trauma is different for everyone. You need to reassure her that she's safe. Meg's ready to blow a hole in the walls until she can find a way out of here. She's terrified and not in the right frame of mind to do anything."

"She can't go on the mission like this," the demon piped up from around the corner, "I can go in her stead, Mia."

"But who will go in my place?" Mia asked, her emotions warred across her visage. She was the one in charge of the mission, she had to go. Yet, the shifter was torn. She wanted to take the witch back to her room and hold her until she calmed down.

"Allow me to take care of her." Eve stated. The shifter eyed the psychic, causing her to look at her feet in shame, "I know much about what she's going through."

"*You* think that I can't save her?" Mia snarled, causing the psychic to flinch.

"No, I don't," Eve meekly stated, "You see her as though she's in danger and all you want to do is find the closest threat to her because of your wolf nature. That's not what she needs and deep down, you know. I'm not a threat to you or her."

"I don't like this," Mia grumbled.

"It's not about you, it's about her and what she needs. Meg is a rude and gruff witch, but she showed me a kindness when I got here. She's been hard, but good to me. Let me return a favor?" Eve pleaded her case.

"Stop talking about me like I'm not here, damnit!" Meg demanded as the shifter let her go. She glared at everyone as she slowly turned in a circle, her magic thrumming and at her command. "Do you think that I'm a weak idiot? I love it here and you'll *not* be taking my home from me again!"

"Meg, no one is doing that," Mia answered as tears streamed down her face.

Eve sat down on the cold concrete floor with her head pressed against her knees, crying. The witch looked down at the psychic, wondering what was happening to her. She kneeled down by her as she rubbed her back, "Don't tell me that they're kicking you out too?"

"No," Eve bit out between sobs, "Emotional overload. Too. Much. To. Bear."

Meg grabbed the psychic protectively and commanded, "Step back. She's hearing us all!"

Everyone moved back, hoping it would, as Mia replied, "Mental shielding up! You too, Meg!"

The witch nodded as she focused on building an impenetrable barrier in her mind's eye. She noticed that her emotions were all over the place and now felt bad for Eve.

She shouldn't have to suffer because I got lazy.

"*You're not lazy,*" Eve mentally spoke to the witch, "*It's my fault I'm like this. Don't feel bad about it.*"

"You're my friend, little miss know-it-all," Meg said out loud, "I failed you. I told you that I would keep my barrier up to keep you from my emotional baggage. I can't even do that right!"

Mia stepped forward, but stopped as a hand on her shoulder held her back, "Let Eve do this for her."

Meg glanced over her shoulder and saw the Fae warrior that's been training with Eve. He, along with Moneek, were the ones responsible for her and Red Jayne finding this place and he had the emotions of a corpse. The witch looked back at the psychic and asked, "Why didn't you tell me?"

"You're reacting to your trauma and not thinking right. Kind of like how I get at times. Everyone is worried about you, especially your furry companion."

Both Meg and Eve snorted and laughed, confounding everyone else. Mia looked at the Far warrior and he impassively shrugged his shoulders, "She's talking and Meg is listening."

"You need to go with her. This is a big deal, your first time leaving here. Just know that I understand what you're feeling and thinking. Fal'destion has been sneaking me outside, trying to aid me." Eve looked up at the witch with watery, bloodshot eyes, *"I feel like a failure to him and now, you."*

"But you're not a failure," Meg spoke. She glanced at everyone, glaring, "Do any of you think otherwise?"

Chapter Sixteen

A chorus of no's filled the corridor as both Axel and Victor approached. They glanced uncomfortably at each other as the larger shifter spoke, rubbing the back of his muscular neck, "So, is the mission scrubbed? What's going on?"

The vampire smirked, "A meltdown that would make Chernobyl look like a campfire."

"Piss off, fang boy!" Meg hissed which caused Victor to laugh.

"Are we going out or having a pity party tonight?" The vampire asked as he crossed his arms behind his back, grinning.

Before Mia could say a word, Meg hopped up and barked, "Yes, we are, but if you want to hang back and share your feeling with the rest of the group, I'll understand." She stormed past the scowling vampire and stuck her tongue out at him, "Undead crybaby!"

Victor turned and grabbed Meg. He tossed her over his shoulder and quipped, "If we wait for her to get to the garage, we might as well stay here. Come along, witch, and no spewing."

Meg snarked as she smacked Victor's back, "I'll be sure to cover us both in vomit. You have crap taste in clothes. A splash of color would do wonders for your complexion!"

"You do and I'll rub your face in it, like a bad dog that just pissed in my coffin." The vampire replied with an evil grin. Mia snarled as Victor slapped Meg's ass, "We'll see you at the garage. Try to keep up people."

The vampire laughed all the way as the world around the witch zoomed by in a blur. She closed her eyes to keep from getting sick, but it didn't help this time. Meg leaned her head next to Victor's shirt collar and threw up just as he stopped by a long, black SUV.

"For fuck sake, woman!" The vampire hissed as he sat her down in front of him. Meg paled as she spewed on his vest. Victor backed away, as if he was being burned by a fire breathing dragon.

"I told you," Meg smirked as she wiped her mouth with the back of her hand, "don't carry me like that. You should go clean up. You reek."

"The vampire grumbled through gritted teeth as the others came inside the garage, "This isn't over, witch. I'll be back momentarily!"

Everyone hastily moved away from the door to let Victor rush by. Mia made a face as the smell of vomit wafted up to her nostrils, "I guess that we have a little more time before we leave."

"Yeah, I'm thinking he's going to need a shower. I got plenty down inside the back of his shirt." Meg giggled.

"Great," Axel said as he walked over to the SUV and opened the back hatch, "Victor's going to be in a mood. Thanks for that, Meg."

"No problem," the witch answered with a grin, "I did warn him. You all heard me, right?"

Mia came over to her and brushed a tuft the witch's hair behind her ear, "Are you okay,

Meg? Do you feel up to going out on this mission?"

Axel walked over and handed Meg a bottle of water and quipped with a grin, "Rinse your mouth out. I don't want to be smelling your witch's breath in the car."

Meg stuck her tongue out at the giant shifter as he walked around and got behind the wheel. Black Jack cried out as he climbed in the front passenger seat, "Shotgun!"

"I guess that we get the backseat," Mia purred and winked. She opened the side door and climbed inside as Meg took several gulps of water. She gurgled and swished some more water in her mouth before spitting it in a utility sink. The witch walked back over to the SUV and slid in next to her shifter.

"I'm sorry about springing this mission on you." Mia said as she looked at the witch with concern.

"It's all good, just give me more of a heads-up next time," Meg replied. She looked down at her feet and sighed heavily, "I don't know why I did what I did. It's not like me to freak out."

"We'll figure it out, together." Mia replied.

A blur of black and a slight gust of wind let everyone know that the vampire had returned. He casually set down in the backseat, next to the witch, staring ahead.

"So, what's upchuck?" Black Jack spouted off as he looked in the rearview mirror at Victor. He fumed as Meg doubled over laughing.

"Can we go now, Axel?" Victor groaned.

Axel picked up a remote, punched in a six-digit code, and the main garage door opened. He put the SUV into gear and pulled out. Meg looked at the vampire and noticed that he still had dripping wet hair. He closed his eyes, trying to relax, but the witch could tell that he was wound up tighter than a screw in a stud. Meg felt a little bit of guilt, but at the same time, she did warn the man.

"What exactly are we doing?" The witch asked.

"Avoiding you and your projectile vomit," Victor hissed but kept his eyes shut.

"Save your anger for the Ferals or whatever nasty entities we run into, Victor," Mia ordered, which he only grunted. The shifter looked at Meg and answered, "We got a lead on more survivors. Apparently, the small cluster is hiding out downtown, in the Shanghai tunnels. I'm not sure if they're still there or not, but we have to try and bring them to the facility."

"I can scout the tunnels for you..." Eric appeared in front of Meg, causing her to flinch. The spectre smirked, *"What's wrong, Meg...? You look like you've seen a ghost..."*

"Careful," Victor warned, "she might spew on you if you keep scaring her."

"Piss off, both of you!"

"Eric, that's a great idea," Jack said, "I don't know about the rest of you, but I'm not looking forward to going in the tunnels."

"Too creepy for you, sorcerer?" Axel asked with a smile.

"No, I'm claustrophobic."

Meg felt confused, "I don't get it. The Shanghai tunnels aren't that tight of squeeze. There's plenty of room to roam around down there."

Black Jack twisted in his seat, facing the witch, "I know this, but even so, I can't go in there. I tried it once around Halloween for the ghost tour and I was only down there for a few minutes before I freaked out. Kind of like you did when you were told we were going out tonight."

"Nice to know this now," Mia grumbled as she glared at the sorcerer, "Why am I only finding out about this now?"

"I... I don't like to talk about it," he looked at everyone, "I don't want you to think I'm a chicken or badly of me."

"There's nothing wrong with fear, boy," Victor announced as he opened his eyes, "Everyone is afraid of something. There's no shame in it. I'm sure that we can accommodate you by not sending you in."

Jack turned in his seat, facing forward with his arms crossed, "I don't want to be sidelined either. I can help in other ways, just not down there."

"We might not even go down there," Meg assured the sorcerer as she touched his shoulder, "Eric can scout it for us so we can know if those people are still down there. I can't wait to see you apply your button mashing skills on the Ferals."

"*I will go there now...*" The ghost stated as it disappeared.

Meg sat back and watched the world pass by under the heavy blanket of night. It all seemed quiet and peaceful. A light rain decorated the windows of the SUV. She curled up next to Mia as memories of the last time she was out in Portland.

So many needless deaths and senseless killings, was this the new normal, Meg wondered.

Mia smiled down at the witch, noting that she was clinging to her body. The shifter gently ran her fingers through Meg's hair as she leaned over and kissed the top of her head.

"I won't let anything happen to you, Meg. I promise."

Meg remained impassive and didn't speak, but the vampire did, "You shouldn't make promises that can easily be broken. She needs to face the danger head on and know that she can and will get hurt."

"I mean what I say, Victor!" Mia snarled, "I'm not letting my little witch out of my sight."

"That's nice and romantic of you, that possessive, protective streak you have, but the fact remains that you can't predict how these missions will turn out. Meg could die if she doesn't realize that she has to protect herself first and not rely on a wolf shielding her from everything."

"I know, but I-"

Victor cut off the shifter, "I'm not trying to provoke you nor tell you what to do. I'm pointing out a hard fact of reality, one that I'm hoping she understands. What say you, witch?"

"Life sucks. Death is the new reality. I may get hurt," Meg looked over, eyeing the vampire intently, "but with everything that I've been taught, I plan on making sure that whomever attacks me *will* experience a pain like they never knew existed."

Axel shuttered, "I can attest that Meg has the power to do that. I don't know what exactly it is, but I sure as hell don't want any part of it again."

"See, wolf?" Victor smiled benevolently, "This is what she needs to have. The mindset of a warrior. If she can't perform like one, then she won't survive. You can't hide her from reality and expect her to do nothing. She has a strong will that will serve her well."

"Must be nice to be an unstoppable creature, with so few ways to die," Mia replied bitterly.

"Nobody is perfect like me, in that respect, my dear," Victor grinned.

Chapter Seventeen

Axel swerved the SUV several times, trying to avoid running over the mutilated bodies that littered Mcloughlin Boulevard. Shadows shifted in the dark just beyond the illumination of the headlights by the different businesses. He turned and went up the Burnside Bridge.

A few vehicles sat quietly on the bridge; each one told the terrible fate of the occupants. Blood was caked on some, while others had the glass broken out. Axel pressed the automatic door lock button, just to be on the safe side.

The SUV crawled over the bridge as stealthily as possible, trying not to draw attention. Black Jack held his dagger in hand, readying himself in case they came near any Ferals. As the SUV crested and slowly descended down, Eric reappeared in the vehicle.

"There's only four people down in the tunnel...I told them that help was coming...The Ferals are down there too...They're being hunted

and herded towards a larger group of Ferals by the Couch entrance..."

"Axel," Victor said, "stop here and let me out." He glanced at the witch and humorously added, "I'm going to pretend that they threw up on me and punish them accordingly."

Axel brought the SUV to a complete halt near the entrance to Chinatown. Victor opened the door and gracefully stepped out. Before he closed the door, the vampire had a playful yet menacing grin as he said, "Happy hunting, children. Don't get killed Meg or I'll never hear the end of it."

He closed the door and sped off before anyone could reply. Axel hit the automatic door lock button as he drove a little way before turning down Third Street. Meg sat up fully, her senses piqued as she could feel the malevolent, crazed stares cast their way.

Mia let out a low growl, preparing to shift, pulling her clothes off. Jack let a long low whistle out in approval. Meg shook her head, "Pig."

"What?" The sorcerer replied, innocently grinning, "I'm just appreciating the show."

"Just so you know," Axel smirked as he leaned next to him, "Mia takes this world's fairy tales seriously. She's a wolf that eats little pigs, like you."

"In that case, I got my dagger so I can free myself from her belly," Black Jack cackled as he flashed the blade so that it glinted in the ambient light.

Meg reached over and opened the door, letting the wolf out. She stroked the wolf's fur as she stepped out of the vehicle. The witch took several deep, calming breaths as she opened her third eye sight which allowed her to see better in dark.

Meg was used to using it to see and commune with otherworldly entities, but with everything that has happened with the Reset, the witch was taught that it has other uses by Adoy, such as night vision.

She was amazed by the clarity it gave everything around her, it was like having a moonlit night with barely any shadows. The flip side was that she could spot the Ferals with ease, which caused her anxiety to kick in. She felt a hand on her shoulder and saw it was Axel, stark naked.

He reassured the witch, "We can have fun with the freaks up here or in the tunnels. Your call, Meg."

The witch did her best to calm her nerves, but seeing the crazed people again made it difficult. Confused, she looked up at the giant shifter, "Why's it up to me? My choice would be to hide in my room with several cases of wine until all this blows over."

"Because there's a good chance that no one is being rescued from the tunnels below. They could all be dead or worse by now. Question is: which scumbags are we ending first, the creeps up topside or the ones below our feet?"

"I think it would be prudent to lay those Ferals to rest," Jack pointed at a growing cluster, "I can protect the entrance, but I'd like their numbers thinned out. Victor will be my backup once he's done playing with the ones on Couch St."

Meg nodded; the conjurer had a valid point. She rolled her shoulders and strolled forward, "It settled. Let's kill these pricks, save the damsels in distress, and then save the world. You going to shift, Axel or are you fighting freestyle?"

Axel grinned as his body contorted and changed, his muscular structure shifted and, to the witch's surprise, got bulkier and thick like leather. Fine, coarse gray hair sprouted across his entire body, except on his face, abdomen, hands, and feet.

Before both Meg and Black Jack stood an upright gorilla, towering over them at almost eight feet tall. Howls from the Ferals reached them as a swarm rushed at them. Jack held up his crimson dagger and said, glancing at Axel, "It's on like Donkey Kong!"

Meg's body pulsated with magic as she screamed, "Charge!"

Mia howled as she ran into the crowd, Axel, despite being a gorilla, moved just as fast and on two legs. His massive arms cleaved through the Ferals like hairy clubs. Black Jack's eyes glowed crimson as he slashed and stabbed sigils at any of the incoming crazed people. Ferals cried out in pain and agony as each sigil hit their intended targets.

"Foul creatures! The whole lot of you!" A Feral woman snarled as she encroached on Meg, her hands were caked in semi-dry blood and most of her clothes were barely covering her scratched and bruised body. A stark testament to the carnage she wrought on innocent victims, like the witch.

Thinking about her first experience only fueled Meg's rage. She dropped into her fighter's stance, her fists balled up and ready to strike. The crazed female chuckled hoarsely, circling the witch, "Kitty has claws. I love playing with my food before I devour it. You will be digesting inside me and I'll make sure you watch it all play out."

"That's a bold statement from a piss poor skank. Let's dance, bitch!"

The Feral woman growled as she lunged at the witch. Meg smiled as a thought occurred to her. She grabbed a hold of the crazed woman, pushing her magic into her as she commanded, "If you're so hungry, then eat yourself! I'm sure that you taste wonderful."

The woman froze in place and stopped fighting. Meg could see her black eyes glazed over as she lifted her forearm to her lips and bit down. Blood gushed as the Feral woman ate more of herself, seeming to enjoy her own flesh and muscles.

Before fully letting her go, Meg added, "Stupid cow! Feet first. They taste better and work your way up."

The Feral woman dropped down on the street and did as she was ordered. She grunted in pain as she tore each toe off, but had a blissful smile as she chewed.

"Remind me *not* to piss you off, witch," Black Jack called out, feeling queasy seeing the crazed female literally eating herself.

Meg grinned as she ran for two more Ferals trying to get to Mia as she ripped out a guy's throat. The wolf snarled as one grabbed her by her tail, dragging her off the prone Feral. She turned and saw Meg place her hands on their backs and commanded, "You shall die now. No one but me makes my wolf howl."

The Feral pair froze, their eyes glazed, before crumpling on the street, clutching their chests. Mia nodded at the witch before rushing after another target. The witch turned and was tackled by three Ferals. One of them pinned down her arms above her head as others groped her body, trying to remove her clothes.

"You're powerless without your hands, so enjoy your painful death."

Fighting through her fear and the memories of trauma, Meg bit out as she flooded her crazed assailants, "Think again, assholes! Kill each other! The winner will kill other Ferals!"

Meg scrambled out from underneath them and hopped to her feet as the Ferals proceeded to viciously attack one another. The witch dusted herself off and looked around for the next threat. Axel had two Ferals up in the air, his massive hands firmly gripping the top of their heads. He roared as he squeezed on their craniums, a sickening pop and snap followed as he crushed their heads like beer cans.

Black Jack managed to down three more Ferals, sweat glistening on his ebony skin. Meg never got around to asking if he had the moniker Black because of his skin or if it was game related. It felt like a taboo subject to broach, despite his laid-back nature. She felt something warm brush against her leg. Mia stood next to her, looking up at her in her wolf form. Her maw was covered in blood and gore.

Meg kneeled down and hugged the wolf tightly as a swift gust of wind blew in. The witch looked up and saw Victor looming over her, his hands dripping with blood. His clothes were remarkably unsoiled and in pristine condition.

"Did I miss anything," he grinned, revealing crimson fangs.

Meg stood up and asked, "What's the status of the Couch entrance?"

"Dead and gory," the vampire quipped, "They never knew what killed them because I'm *that* good."

The witch rolled her eyes, "Your ego matches the bravado. Can you stay with Black Jack and cover the entrance while we locate the survivors?"

Mia shifted into her human form, "No. Axel will stay up here with the sorcerer. We need Victor with us in the tunnels for his speed and stealth."

"I'll keep him safe, Meg. Don't fret," Axel spoke, still as a gorilla.

Confused, the witch blurted out, "Why does he get to walk upright like me and you have to be in full animal style? What gives?"

"It's a choice," Mia replied as she bent down and washed her face in a nearby puddle, the rain came down harder, "I can do what he does, but there's times when I would rather go as a wolf on all four legs. I feel faster, but I'm fast on two legs too. Down there, I plan on being on two legs for better maneuverability."

"I see," Meg said as Mia walked over to her. She kissed her on her cheek and sauntered back to the SUV. The witch shook her head, "I'm so damn clueless."

"Ignorant is more like it," Victor said as he walked over to Hobo's Restaurant. He leaned down and effortlessly lifted open the double steel doors on the sidewalk, "but with time and willingness to learn, that can change."

As everyone gathered at the entrance, the vampire smiled, "After you, children."

Meg motioned to the stairs, grinning, "Age before beauty, fang boy."

Chapter Eighteen

Victor pouted as he jumped down into the hole. Meg rolled her eyes as she stepped down on the ladder, the rungs creaked under her weight. As the witch got to the bottom, Mia started her descent into the tunnel. Meg was disappointed that the shifter had clothes on, but it didn't prevent her from ogling her ass as it swayed with each step.

"We'll keep the entrance doors open, just in case an emergency exit is needed," Axel called down to the others.

Meg looked around, wondering which way to go when Eric appeared. He pointed his ethereal arm and said, "*This way will lead you to the survivors...I will say that you won't be alone in the tunnels...*"

"How many Ferals did you see?" Meg asked.

"*Enough to make this place a death trap...Better yet, a tomb...*"

"It will be a tomb when we're done down here," the vampire stated as he walked away. Mia stepped off the ladder and stumbled into the witch. She smiled warmly as she interlocked her arm with the witch.

They walked quietly, trying to keep their presence unknown to the Ferals. Meg stumbled several times because the ground was packed dirt and uneven in spots. Eric moved next to Victor and whispered, *"I'll let the survivors know you're coming...If I don't return by the time you hit the first junction, three lefts and two rights..."*

"Noted," the vampire muttered with a nod as the spectre disappeared.

Meg kept looking to her left and right, every shadow, nook and cranny could hide a nasty secret, ready to attack. Her skin beaded with sweat despite the cool, musty air in the tunnels. They turned down several paths as Eric reappeared. His face showed panic as he shouted, *"The Ferals have them cornered... They don't have much time...Make haste..."*

Victor turned his head and stated over his shoulder, "Two more rights, ladies. I'll occupy them until you arrive. Be prepared for runners."

The vampire sped off before they could reply. Meg looked at Mia as she let go of her arm. The shifter changed into her wolf form, hair sprouting everywhere that clothes didn't cover. As her lupine snout extended, she growled at the witch, "Don't...be...frightened...Meg..."

Meg watched as the shifter's body grew bigger and taller, her loose-fitting clothes strained under the transformation. Mia looked at the witch and growled, "Piggyback me, now!"

Meg jumped, but did as she was told. She climbed up onto Mia's broad back, holding on tightly as the wolf sprinted down the corridors. Meg inhaled deeply, taking in the sweet scent of cedar, sage and damp fur. She found herself loving this version of Mia just as much as her four-legged form. She stroked the wolf's fur, feeling a sense of peace.

Screams echoed from the tunnel ahead as they turned right, Meg wasn't sure if it was from the Ferals or the survivors. Mia slowed as she sniffed the damp air. She glanced at Meg, "Down, witch!"

Meg slipped down just as several crazed people turned the corner. Mia howled as she charged at the Ferals, slashing at anyone who came close to her. The witch strolled forward; her anger intensified. The magic within her hummed, begging to be unleashed. She reached for the closest Feral, but she stepped in a divot in the ground. Her ankle rolled under her weight, causing the witch to fall on the ground.

As Meg tried to get up, her face met an incoming shoe twice. The witch yelped as she toppled over onto her back, her legs tucked under her body. The Feral man reached down and grabbed a handful of the witch's slick black hair, yanking Meg painfully to her feet. She tasted blood in her mouth as it trickled down from her nose.

"You're coming with me, beautiful," the Feral man growled next to her cheek, his hot breath nearly made Meg vomit. The man attempted to drag her away, but paused as a large wolf towered over the pair.

"Release her now!" Mia roared, her bloody claws twitching.

Meg groaned as she focused her on her magic and commanded, "Let me go and offer your throat willingly to *my* wolf, *now!*"

The witch felt Feral's entire body relaxed as he let her go, causing her to drop down on her knees. The crazed man stepped forward obediently to the wolf and held back his head, exposing his neck. Mia roughly grabbed the man by his upper arms and lifted him off the ground.

The shifter savagely bit into the crazed man's neck. She ripped most of it out in one bite, nearly taking his head clean off. She let the dead Feral drop in a heap at her feet.

Meg wiped the blood off her face as Eric reappeared. The ghost hastily uttered, "*Hurry you two...The vampire is struggling by himself...*"

"Are you saying that the Ferals are besting him," Meg asked.

"*No, they're all dead...A rift opened up and terrible creatures are coming through...He needs assistance...*"

Mia turned and ran down the tunnel. The witch half ran, her foot screamed with pain, but she did her best to ignore it. Her mind wandered at the thought of what could give a vampire trouble in a fight. The witch heard the familiar howl from Mia as she turned the corner.

Meg saw Victor break the neck of a strange, but menacing looking creature. It had dark green, leathery muscular skin and scantily dressed in animal hide on its pelvis. The creature had tiny yellow eyes and a maw that had, what appeared to the witch, to be tusks.

Meg could see the rift wisp in the air like a tear, it pulsated as more of the same kinds of creatures pushed through with deadly large swords. The witch barely sidestepped a body splitting hack from a smaller creature, the blade got wedged into the ground. Meg rushed at it as the creature struggled to free its weapon and punched it in its meaty face several times.

The creature snarled as it grabbed Meg by her neck, her eyes bulged as it cut off her air supply. It lifted her off of her feet and slammed her body down on the packed dirt.

Meg saw little black spots as she gasped for oxygen. The creature stood with its legs planted on either side of her body.

It had managed to dislodge its weapon from the ground and thrusted the blade down at the witch as it growled, "Hold still so I can skewer you, nasty human girl!"

Meg rolled on her side as the blade sliced into her back, causing her to yelp. She felt her body touching the creature's leg and she commanded her magic, "Die ugly!"

The creature paused for a moment, feeling the magic entering its body before replying, "You need to do better than that, girl!"

Undeterred, Meg kicked the beast in the groin. The creature dropped down on the witch, pinning her to the ground. It got into her face, spittle dripped from its maw as it groaned in pain, "You want to play rough, I can-"

Meg watched as two hands grabbed the beast by its bulbous, pig-like head and twisted it. She saw Victor shove the dead creature to the side and, to the witch, he looked more terrifying and deadly. His eyes were blood red and his fangs extended further out than normal. His fingernails extended into claws and were covered in blood and gore.

He effortlessly lifted the witch to her feet and handed her a small sword, "Your magical touch won't affect these orcs, witch, but *this* certainly will!"

Meg nodded as she got in front of the survivors, protecting them from several orcs. One managed to drag a woman from behind and viciously bit into her neck, its tusks gored into the soft flesh and pulled a chunk of muscle out.

"No!" Meg cried out. Her magic was channeled into the short sword, causing it to glow slightly. She slashed and hacked away at the orc; each blow found its mark. The creature doubled over onto the ground, writhing in agony. Meg easily pierced its heart.

Mia stepped up beside the witch and growled, "We need to leave. There're too many orcs! Victor, with me! Meg, help them get out of here!"

Meg nodded as she looked at the weary survivors, "You heard the wolf! Come!"

As she let them get in front of her, Meg heard the feminine voice of the Protector in her head say, "*Close the rift, witch, or this city will be overrun with orcs.*"

Eric appeared at that moment and said, "*Deal with the rift...I can escort these people to the right path out of here...*"

The survivors seemed leery of the spectre, but Meg reassured them, "It's okay, he's with me."

As they fled with Eric, the witch turned her gaze upon the rift. She took a deep breath and focused on it, trying to will it closed, but nothing happened. She groaned as several more orcs came through.

"Keep them off me. The Protector thinks that I can somehow close that damn hole!" Meg called out, feeling a little overwhelmed. The idea of failure flooded her mind.

Victor snapped another neck and picked up two orc swords. He snarled, his hunger evident, "I'm going to need a lot of blood after this is all said and done."

"You can take it from me if we survive this fight," Meg replied. The vampire grinned, flashing his deadly fangs as he beheaded an orc, never taking his eyes off the witch.

What if I can't do it? What if I get us all killed?

"*The power to do it is within you,*" the Protector soothingly spoke, "*Allow me to guide you, witch.*"

"Easy for you to say, I don't know what I'm doing. Why can't you do it for us? After all, you're *the Protector*, right?"

"*It's not my place, child!*" The Protector impatiently hissed, "*Now isn't the time to go over the rules. Now, allow me to guide you or let these creatures run free. Eventually you'll have to deal with them. Your choice, Meg.*"

The witch cringed as she focused on her magic once more, "Okay, what must I do?"

"Use your magic as if you were mending a tear in a piece of cloth. Worm it into the rift and stitch it back together."

Meg's skin tingled as she pushed it out, directing it at the rift. It pierced into the rift, but not enough to push through it.

"Summon more power to you. Your magic needs to be stronger than this. Draw from the Earth. Let your instincts guide you. They make you who you are!" The Protector pressed.

Meg knew she needed to ground herself to the Earth in order to easily draw from it, but she didn't want to be sitting down. The witch imaged her roots sprouting from her feet, instead of her tailbone. It felt strange but in a good way, the power coursed throughout her entire body.

Once more, Meg focused on the rift, as well as on her magic. The boost she received from the Earth was almost overwhelming, causing her to cry out. Victor and Mia turned their attention to the witch as they stopped several more orcs, both watched as she lifted herself up in the air.

Meg's eyes, which were normally a crystal blue, glowed as green as the numerous trees in the Pacific Northwest. One smallish orc came through the rift, its beady eyes grew wide at the sight of the witch. As the vampire slashed at it, the orc ran back into the rift.

Meg used tendrils of her magic to seal the rift, weaving effortlessly into it with little resistance.

"Keep it up, witch. You're almost done." The Protector encouragingly spoke. Meg could feel something pushing against her weaving, trying to get through. She smiled, feeling more confident than before.

"Confidence in yourself and your abilities will go a long way. You may yet make a fine witch, Meg."

A blast of dark energy squeezed through the tiny hole at the top of the rift, causing both Victor and the shifter to search their surroundings for whatever it was. The witch yanked on the tendrils and the rift seal, no signs of it remained, except for the dead orcs.

Meg slowly lowered back down to the dirt path, retracting her roots. She swayed slightly, but before Mia could get to her, a dark presence appeared behind her. Meg cried out as the entity wrapped its elongated arms around her. A feminine voice cooed as it leaned its head by the witch's ear, "She's not your mate any longer, witch. You're *mine*."

"Fuck you and release me, *now!*" Meg yelled as she pushed her magic into the creature. Small pieces of thorny vines, decorated with tiny red flowers, fell off the entity, but nothing else happened. It chuckled as Mia circled it with Victor waiting for the opportunity to strike, "That doesn't bother me. In time, you will forget the wolf and be mine."

Mia roared as she lunged for the emaciated female. Both Meg and the creature vanished into thin air.

Chapter Nineteen

"Meg, no!" Mia cried out, desperately sniffing where they stood only a moment ago. She turned to look at Victor, her eyes wild with anguish.

"We will find her, Mia." the vampire assured her, but solemnly added, "But unfortunately for you, this will be difficult and taxing."

"Difficult and taxing?" The shifter snarled, "My *mate* was abducted right before my eyes! Whatever it is, it's so dead."

Victor walked around the crazed wolf. He bent down, never taking his gaze off Mia, and picked up what appeared to be a trimming off a flower bush. He sniffed it and frowned in disgust, "You will get your witch back, but she won't be the same. You need to be prepared for that, when the time comes."

Mia shifted back into her human form and bitterly spat, "What the hell are you talking about, Victor? Is it going to hurt her? Do you know what it was that took her?"

He cast a sympathetic smile, "Our little witch was snatched by a sahkil. More precisely, a pakalchi. Relax, it won't kill her, but I fear that it may kill you without even touching you."

Mia wearily eyed the vampire, "How is that possible? That bitch is lucky it fled when it did. I'm going to rip its heart out and feed it to it before it dies."

"Help me gather these trimmings. We will need them to find it and your mate. Adoy will know how to track it down magically." Mia nodded as she kneeled down and gathered every scrap of trimmings that she could carry. They ran back to the tunnel entrance together. The vampire kept glancing at the shifter, sensing her unrest, but didn't say a word.

They climbed up the rickety ladder and were greeted by Axel. He looked down into the hole and asked, "Where's Meg?"

"Taken by a pakalchi," the vampire gruffly answered.

"A what?" The giant shifter asked.

"We'll explain everything on the way back to the facility," Victor said. He looked around and asked, "Where's Jack?"

"Taken by Dark Fae. It's like they came out of nowhere."

Victor nodded as he opened the door for Mia. She slid inside quietly; her head cast down. Victor saw the three survivors. He debated on running back to the facility, his lust for blood was becoming unbearable. He turned away momentarily, rolled up his sleeve, and bit down on his wrist.

This wasn't going to satisfy the hunger, but he would be able to tolerate the others in the confines of the SUV. The punctures in his skin healed instantly as he rolled his sleeve back down. The vampire got in the front seat; the vehicle was flooded with the enticing aromas of fresh blood pumping frantically.

Axel got behind the wheel and started the engine and put the SUV into gear. He tensely gripped the steering wheel, his knuckles turned white as he spoke, "I tried to save him. I couldn't get to him in time."

"We'll get both of them back. When we find Jack, you can go ape shit on the Dark Fae." Victor said as he rolled his window down to air out the SUV. They drove in silence for a few miles before Mia asked, "Why did it take her? Why not you or me?"

"Meg was preoccupied closing the rift, which made her an easy target. It feeds off the fear and insecurities of failed relationships."

"But our relationship isn't failing," Mia stated, feeling confused, "I'm sure it will starve to death. My witch is too stubborn to fall for her tricks."

"I wouldn't be so sure. Pakalchi can be persuasive creatures," the vampire stated somberly.

Chapter Twenty

Meg dropped on her hands and knees, emptying the contents of her stomach. Everything in this place was black and devoid of life, yet she heard the entity chuckle behind her, it sounded hollow and cold. She glared at it as she stood up and took a swing at its oblong head. The pakalchi disappeared just as Meg's fist was about to hit it.

It reappeared behind the witch, still laughing. Meg turned and got a good look at it and crinkled her nose in disgust. The pakalchi had a long curvy female body, stood at least seven feet tall, and wore no clothes. Its arms were elongated and its fingers resembled long, thorny vines. Below its waist reminded the witch of a blooming cluster of grass and roots with red flowers, like an organic dress.

Its head had a bulbous, round root that circled the top of its head, like a headdress that grew from its cranium. Macabre designs were woven into the hollow center and pulsated with energy. It had a black stripe that crossed over its eyes. Meg found its eyes were more disturbing to look at because more thorny vines snaked out of them.

"Have a seat, *darling*. We have much to discuss," the pakalchi purred, sounding like thick bushels of wheat straw rustling in the wind.

"The hell with that! Why did you take me from my friends? Who are you?"

"I assure you that I will return you to them, but first, a chat." Its fingers stretched out and dragged a chair over in front of the witch, "Sit."

Meg stood behind the chair, defiantly crossed her arms across her chest, "Give me one good reason why I shouldn't come over there and tear you apart, limb from limb?"

"You couldn't accomplish it even if you tried. I'm too fast. Care to try? Be my guest. I wager that if you hit me, I will take you back."

"And if I can't?"

"You sit and we talk. There's much you need to learn."

Meg grinned as she grabbed the chair and tossed it at the pakalchi, catching it by surprise. The creature fell over, the chair breaking on impact. Black ichor seeped out of the lacerations like sap.

"I hit you, therefore, I win the wager," Meg exclaimed.

"I meant with your fist, witch!" The pakalchi hissed, which sounded like a million locusts swarming in a cave.

"It's not my fault that you didn't specify what I had to use. Now, take me back, as you promised!"

The entity laughed, "You're a feisty one, witch. A lot of spirit in you, as well as darkness. I can teach you how to harness it so creatures worse than myself will tremble before your magic."

Meg snorted as the pakalchi stood up, wiggling like a snake, "Sure. You're going to teach me how to fight monsters tougher than you? That's rich. What's to stop me from using your teachings to kill you?"

"I trust that you wouldn't do that to a new *friend*. I'm on your side. I only have your best interest in mind."

The witch held her arm out and waved it back and forth at the elbow while repeatedly making beeping sounds. The pakalchi stared at her, cocking it weird shaped head to the side, "What are you doing, witch?"

"It's my bullshitter alarm. It's picking up on what you just said, the readings are off the charts."

"How quaint," the pakalchi said with a deadpan expression. Its eyes shimmered slightly, "It doesn't change what I said. I'm your only *friend* right now. You know this is true, *don't* you, Meg?"

A tingling sensation assailed the witch's mind. It was fleeting, but her brain felt like it was in a fog. She shook her head and glared at the pakalchi.

"What did you just try to do to me?"

"Nothing, my *darling*," she cooed as she drew closer to the witch. Meg stilled as it wound its vines around her body, each one hovered about six inches away from touching. "But I'm going to show you what you already know to be true."

"What are you- OUCH!"

The witch cried out as the vines coiled onto her body. Tiny, sharp thorn pierced into her flesh. It stung for a moment, then Meg felt a cold sensation coursing through her body.

The witch swayed back and forth, but never fell. The pakalchi embraced her like a lover, its lips barely grazing her ear, "That's it, Meg. Take it *all* in. *See* the truth. *Kill* all those that have betrayed you. *Hurt* you. *Claimed* to love you!"

Meg's speech was slurred, like she had been out pub crawling, "See...what...? Kill...them...why...?"

"You will know what to do, when the right word is said. When you see the visages of your enemies. False friends will seek to destroy me for giving you this knowledge. You have the clarity to know right from wrong. I need you as my *friend* because more evil monsters are coming to this world. They seek an alliance with your enemies and want to see your beautiful home burn."

"Names...of these...things..." Meg asked, trying to break through the strange haze.

The creature slowly pressed its cold lips against Meg's, she snaked her tongue into the witch's mouth. The witch felt her mouth fill with a thick liquid that tastes like bitter almonds. It oozed down her throat as she willingly swallowed the viscous substance.

"You'll know them in time. You have a home here in the *between realms* plane. The ones that you love want you gone. They want you to find your own place because they fear your dark magic."

Images of Mia, Victor, Black Jack and other people flooded her mind, feelings of mistrust and heartbreak intensified. Her anger flared as Axel's face appeared in her mind's eye. The pakalchi pulled back and pressed its forehead against hers. As the dark entity spoke once more, the witch could hear the whispers of another language embedded with her words. The creature's eyes pulsated as it worked its magic on the witch.

279

"That's it, my *darling*. You know who they are. Their lies slip from their tongue and will cut you like a razor. These people can't join forces with the ones that are coming. It's up to you, Meg, to prevent this from coming to pass. I will watch over you from here, but where you go, I can't come. They won't allow me in, but I can still see your progress. Do you understand?"

Grimacing, Meg answered, "Yes... they all...have it... coming..."

"Good girl," the pakalchi purred.

Eric appeared next to the witch. It had a panicked look as he cried, "*Fight it, Meg...! She's poisoning both your mind and body...! Fight back...!*"

The pakalchi eyed the ghost as she released Meg. It snaked out its vines, catching the ghost by surprise. No matter what he tried to do, Eric couldn't escape.

"*Release me, foul beast...!*" Eric demanded.

The pakalchi grinned, revealing a row of black teeth, "My *friend*! An enemy has breached *our* home. *Protect* me, Meg!"

The witch still swayed; her eyes focused on Eric. She charged at the ghost, her magic thrumming inside her. Eric watched in horror as she magically tore pieces of his ethereal form off.

"Meg…!" The ghost pleaded with his charge, *"Stop…! You're killing me again…!"*

"That's it, *darling*. Shred that little monster until nothing remains. You don't want it to hurt your only *friend* in this world, do you?" The pakalchi asked, working its charm on the witch.

"That's not happening!" Meg growled; her pale blue eyes turned a sickly yellow as she tore the ghost to sunder. Eric released one final agonizing groan of pain that echoed within the confines of the *between realms* plane.

Meg fell down on her knees with her eyes closed. She clutched at her chest as she experienced pain, like she had been stabbed in the heart. The pakalchi towered over the witch, a satisfactory smile spread across its visage.

"The pain you feel is natural. When you kill them..." The creature paused, trying to find the right words. She caressed Meg's silky black hair, "You feel what they did to you. I take the worst of it for you. You won't die, but your body will be purged of their toxic influence."

The witch groaned through gritted teeth, "I understand, my friend."

"Good. I believe that it's time to take the fight to them. *Our* enemies have thrown the first punch, it's time to finish what *they* started. I don't want to live in fear of losing *our* home or you, *darling*. Are you prepared, Meg?"

The witch stood up as the pain left her chest. She opened her eyes, revealing the sickly yellow glow. The pakalchi embraced her like a lover as Meg had a malevolent grin, coldly stating, "They'll never see *this* coming. No one hurts *my* friend!"

And with that, they both teleported away.

Chapter Twenty-One

"Eric should've been back by now," Mia growled impatiently. The shifter had been on edge and frantically pacing ever since they returned from the Shanghai tunnels, three days ago. "I don't like this."

"What would you like? He has to figure out where she is first," Victor stated.

"They're connected. Wherever she is, Eric can easily find her. Why hasn't he returned?"

Everyone that was available gathered in the conference room. Teams that returned from their raids had one thing in common: rifts opening up and things spilled through. The number of survivors was growing, but at a cost. Not all the warriors that went out returned. They weren't prepared for a fight on two fronts.

To make matters worse, warriors were being snatched. It's one thing if they fell in battle, but being captured meant more uncertainty of what fate awaits them. Mia was struggling to keep her composure. Every now and then, she would partially shift, her emotions warred inside her mind.

"Adoy, are your tracking spells ready?" Gaylish asked.

"With as many people being snatched," he answered solemnly, "it will take time."

Mia rushed over to the magical master, she towered over him as anger and anguish raged across her face, "Meg doesn't have time to wait! We need to find her and fast!"

Victor put a hand on her shoulder and received a punch to his face. The vampire didn't budge, but effortlessly blocked several more strikes. He wrapped his arms around her, restraining the angry shifter and said, "We will find them all. Meg is your mate, I get that, but you need to be prepared to do something that you don't want to do."

"And what's that, leech?"

"If we can't save her, then death is the alternative for the witch. She's been with the pakalchi far too long. She may very well be lost to us."

"No!" Mia howled. She thrashed around, trying to escape from the vampire's embrace, but failed. "She hasn't been gone that long! We need to find her, now!"

Adoy placed a hand on her leg, sympathy etched into his small face, "Time flows differently here than it does in the *between realms* plane. The pakalchi like residing there because they can manipulate their victims easier. A few hours there is actually like days passing here, which is a long time."

"Send me there," Mia pleaded with a growl, "I'll ferret the bitch out and bring-"

"We have an intruder outside," a gremlin called out as he zoomed the camera in, "Looks like a female dressed all in black walking this way."

Mia's eyes widened, "Meg! It's her! I know that body anywhere!"

"Hmm, this doesn't bode well." Adoy spoke to no one in particular, "If she's returned, then the pakalchi is skulking nearby, probably in the *between realms* plane. Watching and feeding off the witch."

285

"Let me go," the shifter hissed at the vampire, "I must go to her!"

Gaylish put a hand on Mia's shoulder. The shifter eyed the woman, pleading as the leader spoke, "I will let you go to her, but I must caution you. Meg isn't going to be in her right mind. She will more than likely be looking for a fight. We need her distracted long enough to take down the true threat, the pakalchi."

"She's in pain. I can feel it."

"I know that she is, which indicates that the pakalchi has its terrible influence over her mind. We're the enemy, from Meg's point of view, and you will take the brunt of her fury. Just know that in Meg's darkest hour, you will be her salvation once we rid her of the pakalchi's hold. Let her go, Victor."

The vampire let Mia go and she bolted out of the room. Adoy spoke with the others, forming a plan of attack as Gaylish pulled Victor to the side.

"Meg is a powerful witch and under the pakalchi's influence. She can easily decimate the facility."

"This I know. If she can't be reached or brought to heel, I will end her life. I know it's what you're asking me to do."

Gaylish slowly nodded, her lips thinned as she tried to be as emotionally neutral as possible, "I don't ask this lightly. I know you care about her, as a friend. She's an ally we can't lose, but we can't allow her to die a pain-filled, emotional death at the hands of the pakalchi. Make it swift, for Meg's sake."

The vampire curtly nodded as he walked away, "As you command, Gaylish."

Gaylish slumped her shoulders slightly as everyone departed the conference room. She walked over to the monitors and stood behind several gremlins. One looked up at her and asked, "Do you think we can actually save this one? Pakalchi poison will kill her if it goes untreated."

"I know Hugo, which is why I have several options in place. Meg will suffer greatly if she lives through this cat-and-mouse game with the pakalchi." She clasped her hands behind her back and straightened her shoulders, "Only time will tell what fate is in store for our witch."

Chapter Twenty-Two

Meg walked towards the facility. It was huge, but old looking. One would believe it to be abandoned, which was how her former *friends* wanted others to perceive it. Her anger grew as the pakalchi whispered into her mind.

"They don't want you or care about you. They see only power and want to use your abilities for their own gains. No one loves you the way that I do, Meg."

The witch snarled out loud, "Yes. I should just level this building and force them to dig out."

"That's too good of a fate for our enemies. You need to ensure that they die. All of them. You don't want them to come after us? They want to hurt me!"

"Don't worry," Meg replied as the main doors opened, "I'll keep you safe."

People came flooded out, causing the witch to maliciously grin. The pakalchi whispered as the denizens of the facility formed a line in front of her.

"See how they fear your presence? If they meant you no harm, they would let you walk inside."

"Meg, are you all right?" Red Jayne called out.

"I will be when you're all *dead*!" Meg replied, her magic thrumming throughout her body.

"We mean you no harm," the Native American spoke, "Come inside so we can talk."

"No dice, Dan. I can't, in good conscience, let you people join forces with your allies. This ends here and *now*!"

The pakalchi chuckled as Mia stepped forward, tears trickled down her face, "Please Meg! Come back to me! You're not like yourself."

"My friend enlightened me about *all* of you. I'm just your stupid puppet that you wish to use as you see fit. You *never* loved me! You wanted to cast the ignorant witch out, well now's your chance to do so. Who wants to die first?"

Before anyone could reply, the witch released a torrent of magic at the group, knocking Mia and several others down. Meg gasped as she clutched her chest, she angrily glared at Axel, "I'm going to rip your monkey arms off and beat you to death with them!"

She ran at the giant shifter, screaming as her fists glowed black. Axel put his arms behind his back and waited patiently for the witch's assault. The pakalchi whispered, "*He knows that he's done you wrong and wishes to be punished. Take the coward out!*"

"Dan! Jayne! Now!" Mia ordered.

Jayne put her hand out and focused on a spot in the air. Her eyes glowed crimson as she yanked, pulling the pakalchi out of the *between realms* plane. Meg hit Axel with one solid punch to the gut. The strike sent the big man hurling backwards in the air, about five feet, before he crashed hard on the pavement.

Meg ran towards the giant shifter, but stopped as Mia got between the two. Meg snarled as her fist glowed brighter, "Move it, *bitch*. It's his time to die. Go wait your turn!"

"No, this has to stop! I don't know what that *thing* did to you, but I won't let it hurt you or anyone else for that matter."

"You sent Eric to kill us and he paid the ultimate price by *my* hands. You're right, you blonde bimbo, this ends tonight!"

The lovers circled each. Meg's eyes changed from the sickly yellow and were completely black, malice etched into her facial expression. Mia held her hands out in a placating manner, "I don't want to hurt you. I love you, Meg! Fight her hold that she has over you!"

The pakalchi cried out in a panicked voice, "*Meg*! Save me, my *friend*!"

Meg paused and looked over her shoulder. She saw the pakalchi hovering in the air. It released a barrage of thorns at Red Jayne, but Dan blocked the attack. The Native American used his telekinesis and threw the barb projectiles back into the dark entity. It groaned angrily as it sent a torrent of vines, snaring whomever she could reach. The Native American was hoisted into the air by his throat. He dangled helplessly as he desperately clawed at the deadly vine.

Quicker than the eye could track, Gloria cleaved her sword on the vines, releasing Dan, and slashed at the pakalchi's body. Thick black ichor seeped from her wounds as the vampire kept a protective stance in front of the Native American.

"No!" Meg cried out. She dropped to her knees hard, clutching her chest. She glared at shifter and bitterly spat as a black substance trickled from her mouth and nostrils, "You never loved me like *she* does. I *hate* you! I'll fucking kill you all!"

Jayne strained to magically hold the pakalchi, it drew more power from the witch. Mia cried out, desperate for her witch to listen to her pleas, "Fight it, Meg! She's *killing* you!"

Meg screamed as her entire body convulsed, her eyes rolled back into her head. Mia shifted in her wolf form and sprinted straight at the pakalchi. The dark entity glowered as she spoke indignantly, "Foolish creatures! You think you can stop me? The witch is healing me and there's nothing any of you can do to stop me. She's a power source that I *will* drain as I kill all of you!"

Victor stood over Meg's convulsing body, glancing between her and the pakalchi. He bent down and picked up the witch and spoke coldly, "Let's see how you fare without your advantage."

Victor bit down into Meg's neck. It took all of his strength to hold her still so he could feed. The pakalchi hissed as she released more vines, trying to stop the vampire. Gloria swung her sword, severing vines like she was wielding a weed eater.

The pakalchi cried out as it dropped down to the ground, Red Jayne smirked as she energetically gripped the dark entity in place. Mia jumped on top of the pakalchi's snakelike body, causing it to look on in fear.

"Your bitch is as good as dead, wolf. You may slay me but I've-"

Mia viscously bit down into the pakalchi's throat. She ripped so much flesh out that she nearly decapitated the dark entity. Gloria walked over as the wolf spat out the vile flesh and finished removing its head by yanking it off by its circular crown root.

"You want a trophy for your wall?" Gloria asked, her southern drawl pronounced as she held it aloft, black ichor oozing out of its neck.

"All I want is my *witch*," Mia said as she shifted back to normal. She looked over at where she left Meg and saw that the vampire held her as he drank from her neck. The shifter snarled as she stormed over to the vampire, "What the hell are you doing, Victor?"

Victor looked at her as he pulled his fangs from Meg's neck, thick maroon blood caked his lips. Mia saw that his eyes weren't crimson or normal, they resembled the sickly yellow that Meg had, "I did what needed to be done. Gloria, take her to the infirmary, *now!*"

The female vampire flew past Mia before she could get to her mate and did as Victor asked. She glanced at Mia sympathetically before rushing towards the facility. Mia stood toe to toe with Victor, her claws coming out of her fingers.

"Care to explain why you were feeding on *my* mate?"

The vampire's face soured, like he was going to be sick. He pushed past the shifter and ran over to a small patch of grass. Victor released a torrent of the same maroon substance that he ingested from Meg as he dropped down on his hands and knees, his body quaked with each spasm. Mia slowly walked over to the vampire, keeping her claws out in case he turned on her in a fit of bloodlust.

Victor didn't look up as he spewed more, but he held up a hand at the shifter. He wiped his lips on the back of his sleeve, sneering at the substance. He focused on what he evacuated from his stomach, groaning in between breaths, "I did what needed to be done, Mia. She was going to die if her blood wasn't drained out. The pakalchi's hold on her was a deadly one."

"Are - are you going to be okay, Victor?" Mia asked.

The vampire bitterly laughed, "I just bled your mate dry and *you're* worried about *me*? I could've killed her. I easily could've snapped her pretty little neck, but didn't. Have at me, if it makes you feel better about what I did. Just know that I did it for both of you."

"I'm concerned that the need to feed is outweighing your sense of judgement," Mia answered firmly as she could sense his turmoil, "I-"

The vampire quickly snapped his head in her direction, his eyes were full on red. He hissed at the shifter, his fangs extended menacingly, "Go to her and leave me be, damn it! Meg needs you more than this *monster* needs you and your sympathy at the moment."

Mia nodded as she slowly backed away. She retracted her claws and said, "I don't see a monster before me, Victor. I see a friend in pain."

"Clearly, we have different definitions of what a monster truly is," Victor answered coldly as he stood up. He sped off before Mia could reply. She turned on her heels and ran towards the facility. Tears trickled down her face, her emotions overwhelmed the shifter at the thought of what fate awaited the witch.

Meg was securely strapped down on a bed, each cuff had magical runes and sigils embedded in them to nullify the witch's power. Mia gasped when she saw several lines that pumped blood into her body.

How much blood did Victor take?

Jace sat on the bedside, inserting another line for a saline solution. He looked up and saw the shifter.

"Do you think that she will make it?" Mia hesitantly asked as she sat down in a chair on the opposite side of the bed.

"I have no clue. She lost a lot of blood. Plus, there's the poison to take into account."

"Poison?" Mia's eyes widened with fear and confusion, "I don't understand. We killed the pakalchi, did that not sever their connection and end the threat?"

Dr Arnica placed a comforting hand on the shifter's shoulder, "No. According to what Adoy said, Meg is going to have to sweat it out. The blood is helping, but I've had to sedate her so her body could relax as it purges the poison. Victor might've saved her life, but only time will tell. Brace yourself for the worst and hope for the best, Mia."

Mia nodded solemnly. She reached out and grasped Meg's hand as her body twitched and jerked. Moans escaped the witch's mouth.

"Fight this, Meg." Mia firmly spoke, her eyes tearing up once more, "Fight for yourself. I'll always be here. Like I have been, before you knew that I existed."

Jace stood up and turned to leave, but paused at the door. He looked back at the shifter and said, "We're all here for you two. Make sure that you eat and rest. No sense in punishing yourself needlessly."

A single tear escaped her eye, "I failed her. I couldn't even keep her safe. Meg deserves better than me."

Everyone vacated the room, leaving the shifter alone with her mate. Mia wanted to curl up next to the witch, but didn't want to accidentally pull the different IV lines out. It was breaking her heart seeing her witch in this state. The shifter knew that this was a fight she couldn't participate in; it was all on Meg to outlast the pakalchi's poison.

Chapter Twenty-Three

Meg wearily opened her eyes, the dim light from the ceiling stung her vision. She felt worn out, like she had run a marathon while drunk. Her head pounded like a hangover, but this was much worse. She reached down to cover her head with her blanket, but her hands barely budged.

"What the actual fuck?" Meg blurted out, seeing the restraints for the first time.

She tried sitting up, but got knocked back down by the widespread body pain. She howled painfully, feeling like every part of her body was being stabbed by tiny pixies. The witch searched the room and saw that it was devoid of life, yet she heard a female voice just outside the door to her right.

Am I a prisoner? Why not, I deserve to be imprisoned after what I did, especially to poor Eric…

Meg bitterly cried, recalling her actions. *Eric wasn't a friendly ghost, but he didn't deserve to go out like that.* Her emotions ran rampant as she sobbed and wailed. She barely registered a timid hand on her forearm, it squeezed just enough to get her attention. Meg peered through her bleary vision and saw Eve standing next to the bed.

"It's good to see you finally awake. I sensed you coming to, so I called and notified everyone." Eve said, smiling meekly.

"What?" The witch exclaimed; her eyes showed fear. She yanked at her restraints, desperately trying to escape. "Release me, Eve!"

Eve gently moved her hand down and let her fingers touch the restraints, "I can't do that. I know that these aren't comfortable, it never is pleasant for me either."

"Please, Eve. You don't understand," the witch pleaded. She tried calling her magic, but nothing happened. She anxiously eyed the petite woman and asked, "What's wrong with me? My magic is gone! What did I do to it?"

"Nothing. It's the restraints, remember? I was put in these shortly after I arrived here because they neuter magical abilities." Eve

302

sighed heavily, "It seems to be my fate no matter where I'm taken."

Meg nodded slowly, recalling how the young girl's psychic ability became overwhelming, unintentionally hurting people in her wake. Meg managed to use her magic to shield herself from the torrent of Eve's gift to get in close to render her unconscious. The witch felt bad for her, Eve was like a scared rabbit with a nuclear weapon strapped to her back. Eve had her own troubled past, one filled with pain and suffering. Meg promised that she would help her get rid of her demonic tormentor, as did several others. Among them, ironically, was a demon.

The thought of the others made the witch resume her escape attempt; she didn't want to see any of them. It was bad enough that Eve was in the room with her, Meg couldn't recall if she was outside during the fight.

"Since you refuse to release me-"

"I'm not refusing," Eve cut the witch angrily. The young girl barely spoke and when she did, it came out as a whisper. Meg paused, waiting for the psychic to calm down. She was still struggling with her gift, but she was getting better.

At least my head didn't explode like on Scanners, the witch thought as Eve softly spoke.

"I don't have the key or I would've done it by now." She cocked her head, eyeing the witch curiously, "Why do you want the blanket over your head?"

Meg sighed, depression setting in, "You're the psychic, you should already know. I don't-"

The door opened quickly; the many residents of the facility poured through. The witch turned away in shame, averting her eyes from everyone. She didn't want to see their disappointed looks nor their reasonable baleful gazes, especially not from *her mate*.

Before anyone spoke, Eve requested, "Unlock her restraints. She's safe and doesn't want to hurt anyone else or herself."

Meg heard Dr Arnica's confused voice answered, "But, that's not why she's in them. If you say she's okay, then I'm all for it."

The witch felt hands groping around at both her wrists and ankles as Eve softly spoke, "Sorry, it's something that I've heard too often. Condition response, I suppose."

Meg imagined the young psychic was meekly looking away, rubbing her arm. She had seen Eve do it enough in the short time that she was here. Her imagination kept going, the witch didn't want to face the eyes of her friends.

She knew if she did, there would be troubled glares from Black Jack, Dan, and Red Jayne. Axel most certainly would be cracking his knuckles, wanting to take her head off. She heard him say, "You sure? She might be better off like this."

The twins, Victor with crimson, hungry eyes being held back by Gloria. Adoy would be shaking his head with disappointment. And Mia.

Meg didn't want to see her heartbroken eyes, the hurt that she inflicted on her shifter that night. The witch wouldn't be surprised if she wasn't in the room or if she was, bitterly glaring before walking out silently.

Once her hands were free, Meg yanked the blanket up, covering her head. She heard Eve answer the giant shifter, "This part is about trust. Do you trust Meg to a good witch or do you prefer her helpless and powerless because she's an easy target to prey on?"

"What? No, I'm not like that!" Axel growled at the little psychic, which angered Meg, as he whined, "You haven't been on the receiving end of one of her magically charged punches. She broke four of my ribs! Being a shifter means that I recover faster, but bones mending hurts."

"I'll break the rest of your baby back ribs, asshole, if you keep snapping at my friend!" Meg hissed as her magic thrummed through her body once more. Despite her anger, the witch didn't dare uncover herself. Her shame seemed to supplant it and with it, came the guilt.

"At least her cheery disposition is back to baseline," Axel stated as he took six steps back.

"Meg, why are you hiding, dear?" A female voice with a southern drawl asked, which meant it was Gloria.

No response.

Victor calmly remarked, "Come on, Meg. Uncover yourself so we can see how your vampiric transformation is coming along."

Meg sprang up. She flung the blanket off the bed, wide eyed, then she fell back on the bed, moaning in pain.

"Fuck! Is that the reason for the pain?" The witch bit out as she curled up in a fetal position. She ran her tongue over her teeth, probing them for fangs.

Gloria smacked Victor on the back of his head, "See what you did? You should be ashamed."

"I'm far too old for shame in my life. Look, it got her uncovered, didn't it?" Victor remarked with a smirk.

Meg whimpered, "What's causing the pain?"

"It's a side effect of the pakalchi's poison," Dr Arnica interjected, "As I understand it, you're going to feel like this for a few more days. You may feel exhaustion and fatigue, so you're on bed rest."

"Everyone was so worried about you, Meg," Eve said as she sat down on the cold tile floor, getting eye level with the witch. "You may not believe that, but I *know* it to be true."

"But why? I've done terrible things. I attacked this place, hurt others, and..." Meg shook as she gulped hard, "killed my friend."

"No one died while you were possessed," Axel stated, but pointed at his midsection, "but I do know for a fact that you hurt me."

"Stop whining," Mia spoke, causing the witch to flinch. "You're all healed up. Meg has had it way worse than you. You'll get no sympathy here, you big baby."

The witch felt a shift on the bed behind her and knew that it was Mia, her scent wafted to her nose.

Cedar and sage.

Meg enjoyed her scent, but at the same time, guilt flooded her mind. She shivered at the shifter's soft touch across her cheek. Before

Meg could talk, Mia blurted out, "I'm so sorry, Meg. I failed you miserably. This is all my fault. Can you find it in that big, beautiful heart of yours to forgive me, my love?"

"Forgive what? I'm the evil one here, not you. Everyone would be better off if I was dead and no longer a threat. I shredded Eric. I murdered the one that tried to help me. I'm not worth saving nor anyone's pity."

The others murmured to each; Meg didn't bother to listen to their accusatory verbatim. Mia looked at the others, feeling confused, and back at her mate, "You were under the pakalchi's influence. None of us hold what you did against you during that time. Damnit, I should've been quicker to act when she grabbed you!"

"She doesn't see it that way," Eve stated as she rested her chin on the mattress, "Meg sees us as the victims, not herself. More guilt and shame. Meg, you're a victim in this equation. The true culprit is the pakalchi and she's the one that attacked everyone, including yourself."

"We're all here for you, Meg. You're a part of this team. Why do you think we're in here with you?" Dan stated.

For the first time, the witch truly looked at everyone. She half-heartedly snarked with a nervous laugh, "So, no torches and rope. I guess that's a good sign that I'm not going to be burned at the stake."

Mia rubbed the witch's soothingly, "I think she's still feeling the effects of the pakalchi's influence. Its goal is to feed off its victims by forcing them to break any bonds and tear relationships apart. That's why it was so strong and why it struggled when Victor drank her blood."

Meg gasped, "You actually fed on me?"

The vampire slightly shrugged his shoulders, he half smirked and sneered, "To be fair, you did offer yourself willingly to me. I was more than happy to oblige, but your blood was tainted with the pakalchi poison and it didn't sit well."

The witch chuckled, "Aww. Witch's blood gave the big, bad vampire a tummy ache? Did you not enjoy tapping the witch's brewski?"

"Feel better and I might take another sip. It was either I drain you to the brink of death or snap that pretty little neck. *That* was an order that I reserved as a last resort."

Mia glared at Gaylish, but she was unfazed, "Tough options have to be explored. There was a chance that Meg and the pakalchi would be too powerful to stop. I make no excuses. Sometimes the needs of the many outweigh the needs of the few. Who in here would've considered killing the witch?"

"None, Gaylish. Though Axel is still bitter that he got his ass kicked by a girl. Again." Eve commented as she playfully winked at Meg with a sliver of a smile.

Meg nodded slowly, "Being a good leader comes with a baggage cart full of shit. I don't blame you for considering it, Gaylish. We're here together to stop what's going on outside these walls and I became the enemy. Say, where's Black Jack? Is he hiding or did you guys dump him in the tunnels to torment him?"

"He's been snatched. The same time that you were taken. Fal is trying to track him down as we speak." Mia stated as she laid down behind the witch, cuddling her.

Meg nodded, "If he's not back by the time I'm able to move, I want to help with the search."

Meg moaned softly, enjoying the feel of the shifter's warm body against hers. A dark figure appeared behind the petite psychic. The robed female had everyone's attention as she spoke, "This is to be expected. As more darkness floods into this world, you're all on the front line in this fight and also targets to be taken out. Meg was lucky. Black Jack isn't faring any better. The Reset is doing its part, but a greater evil is coming."

Meg thought for a moment, recalling her time with the pakalchi, then asked, "I vaguely remember the pakalchi said that others were coming to form an alliance here. She meant that they were coming here, to be with you guys, but I know that's a lie. Is it true that some ugly nasty fucks are coming here?"

The Protector closed her eyes, concentrating, "Know that I'm the Protector because I sacrificed my mortal self to ensure that humanity had a fighting chance against not only the machinations of your governments, but to save lives for the ultimate war that is to come. The ones that the pakalchi spoke of is a real threat and will look to create their own grand armies to fully conquer this beautiful world."

"So, we have some time before that happens?" Meg asked hesitantly. Her stomach churned as the Protector's eyes opened, her violet eyes glowed brightly. A feeling of dread washed over the witch.

"No, my child. They're arriving here, walking on the Earth as we speak."

Chapter Twenty-Four

Somewhere near the summit of Mt. Hood, a rift opened. A dark figure stepped out and onto the snow-covered outcropping. He sneered as the wind howled all around him. He wasn't accustomed to the frigid weather, but knew it was necessary to be here. From his vantage point, the NightRipper was relieved to see that the rest of the area below was plush and green.

Several more entities walked through the rift, each one grumbling about the cold. The NightRipper couldn't blame them, they were of demonic lineage such as a Barbazu, a Marilith, and a Balor. He hadn't achieved that status, but by the grace of Lamashtu, the NightRipper may receive rank here on Earth. A Lich stepped out, unfazed by the arctic weather. He seemed to relish in the cold, despite receiving baleful gazes from the upper-level demons.

"Who chose this spot to enter from?" The Balor growled, scowling at the snow.

"I don't know," The Marilith answered as it looked at the undead Lich, "but I have my own suspicions."

The Lich smiled; his gaunt, skeletal visage unfazed by the accusation. His deep echoing voice was lit with amusement, "Ever trusting, Semusk. As much as I'd like to claim credit for this spot, I can't. Though, I find it amusing seeing upper-level demons freezing their asses off for a change."

The Barbazu growled as it grabbed the Lich by his neck, dangling him over the precipice of the mountain, "I tire of you. Maybe a long drop and a sudden stop would do you some good."

The Lich cackled without a care for his own safety, "Do it, I dare you! I'll not only survive, but I'll be days ahead of all of you. I hope you can conjure a fire in the snow because it will take all of you a while to descend down this treacherous slope."

"Enough, Krogar!" The NightRipper hissed, his impatience showing, "Put Mazerth down."

"Gladly," The bearded devil grinned as he released his grip, letting Mazerth fall off the side of the mountain. The Lich maniacally laughed as he freefell.

The Balor grumbled, "Can we go, Riktus? I'm itching to raze this world to the ground."

"Move on, Cyndern," The NightRipper answered the fire demon, glaring at Krogar, "Together. That's how this was supposed to be."

Krogar laughed, "Enjoy the long trek down. I won't be waiting for either of you at the bottom." The Barbazu teleported away.

Cyndern grumbled, "The prick could've taken us down with him."

"You expect much, fire demon. Hmph, if I didn't know better, I'd think you've gone soft, like the bearded devil. Can't handle a small walk down a large mountain?" Semuck mocked.

"Not all of us were granted a serpent body. At least you can slither down without much exertion."

Riktus shook his head as he stomped past the bickering demons, "Doesn't matter. Just move on and let's take out our hatred on the denizens of this world. I have an army to raise and people to flay."

The demon lords trekked down Mt. Hood in utter silence, plotting their own personal hell that they want to reign down on the Earth. Each one had a singular shared thought; any that stands against them will beg for a quick death. Something that wouldn't be granted, ever.

Coming soon.

When the Veil Falls

The Reset: Book Two

Other novels by Joshua Griffith

The Yonuh Trilogy

In a World of Darkness

Where Evil Lays Waste

A Beacon of Light Arises

*

The Coming of Hell

*

The Decaying Destiny of Bobby the Zombie

*

Xander Bane Chronicles

Enter the Dampire

Made in the USA
Middletown, DE
10 November 2020

23612856R10179